TERRI RATH

Wings of Starlight

Copyright © 2024 by Terri Rath

All rights reserved. No part of this publication may be reproduced, stored or transmitted in any form or by any means, electronic, mechanical, photocopying, recording, scanning, or otherwise without written permission from the publisher. It is illegal to copy this book, post it to a website, or distribute it by any other means without permission.

This novel is entirely a work of fiction. The names, characters and incidents portrayed in it are the work of the author's imagination. Any resemblance to actual persons, living or dead, events or localities is entirely coincidental.

Terri Rath asserts the moral right to be identified as the author of this work.

Terri Rath has no responsibility for the persistence or accuracy of URLs for external or third-party Internet Websites referred to in this publication and does not guarantee that any content on such Websites is, or will remain, accurate or appropriate.

Designations used by companies to distinguish their products are often claimed as trademarks. All brand names and product names used in this book and on its cover are trade names, service marks, trademarks and registered trademarks of their respective owners. The publishers and the book are not associated with any product or vendor mentioned in this book. None of the companies referenced within the book have endorsed the book.

Second edition

Cover art by Covers by CKB

This book was professionally typeset on Reedsy. Find out more at reedsy.com

For the ones just as odd as myself

Contents

Preface		ii
Acknowledgments		iv
1	The sting of a bee	1
2	Bargains, trades, and an offering	7
3	A luminous thread	17
4	An insurmountable distance	22
5	Water and fire	25
6	Wings of darkness	31
7	Confessions of madness	36
8	Matters of the heart	41
9	A cold voice	46
10	All of the heavens	49
11	The touch of a mortal	52
12	Entwined	57
13	A fallen Star	61
14	Stinky-fish and honey bread	66
A Lingering Dream: The Celestial Sagas, Book one		75
Excerpt from Dancing for the Cold Moon		78
A word from the author		80
About the Author		81
Also by Terri Rath		82

Preface

If you are familiar with my work, you will know that my stories tend to spiral into dark trauma. So, I am quite pleased to present a love story with only some mild trauma. Ha!

This novella is set long before the events in *A Lingering Dream*, while connected, it is a stand-alone story that can be read in any order. I had not planned on this little side quest—as I have at least three books needing to be written, but my brain kept asking me, "What would happen if a crow fell in love with a star?" Thus, this story was formed. The first edition was released in October 2024, and the story was so well received, that I decided to expand it to release a second edition with in-depth lore which ended up being triple the wordcount from the first edition.

I hope you all enjoy this side story within the Celestial Sagas series as much as I did writing it. Happy reading, lovelies!

A note to readers: I would like to state that I did not attempt to appropriate from any cultures, and I apologize if my story is perceived in such a way. It is never my intention to appropriate, and I always hope to honor any cultures from which I may pull inspiration. I welcome any discourse if you feel that I have done a disservice to my readers. I will strive to learn from and correct any issues that I feel is necessary.

TW/CW: Please take any needed precautions as you read. This work has many sensitive topics, including but not limited to:

- Sexual content
- Fantasy violence in the form of physical assault
- A death
- Hints of suicidal ideation

Acknowledgments

I wish to thank my muse, Vero. You carry the other half of my brain that works, and I am blessed to have you as a kindred spirit.

Of course, thank you to all of my wonderful supporters and dedicated readers, I could not carry on without you!

As always, thank you to my dear friend, C.K., every comma in this book was put in because of you. Ha! Please check out her wonderful stories.

https://www.ckbeggan.com/

And lastly, with the fullness of my heart, thank you to my eternally patient soulmate, and to my Wild Child for giving me the space and all the snacks I needed to create. I do this in the hopes that one day we will have enough financial freedom for you both to live out the dreams hidden within your spirits without being bound to the tethers of this earth. I love both of you forever!

1

The sting of a bee

The gods must have laughed when they placed one such as myself on a little green island full of warriors. For you see, from the moment I was born into this realm, I have been marked as different—both in form and spirit.

My people are a fiercely proud clan of fighters who place much value upon battle prowess and hardened bodies. But alas, I am a soft-hearted creature who prefers beauty over bloodshed, even becoming a Craftsman at an early age. Well...not quite. In truth, my people say that I am merely a tinker because my creations are of no import, thus I am not worthy to be accorded such an honored title. No matter, I continue despite their disdain for my work.

My interests alone marked me as peculiar, but I did what was expected of me, learning the skills needed to defend our homeland from invaders who envied the fertile soil beneath us, even becoming an excellent bowman at a young age, much of it due to my unusually keen eyesight.

The greater mark of my difference is my physical form. I possess the dark hair and skin of my people but that is all. The majority of the peoples here are of middling height with brawny bodies; whilst I grew to be the tallest in the entire village, and lithe with hands designed for more delicate things than weapons of war.

Now, my cousin, Jak, is swarthy, tactical, and unmatched in physical combat, which naturally led to him becoming a leader of the younger warriors. Therefore, he is looked upon as the ultimate specimen among our clan causing many of the young men and women to hope for a match. However, since he lost both of his parents in the Flower wars, it is up to his guardian, my mother, to approve his choice of lifemate and she has not yet agreed upon an arrangement with any of the families despite many invitations.

It is common for people to mistake Jak as my mother's son, since both are great warriors of renown with many shared physical qualities. As a boy, I sometimes wished that *he* were the blood son, and *I* the orphan cousin, so I would not be such a disappointment when I failed in every way to emulate my mother.

As if my gangly form was not enough to mark me an outsider, the gods gave me blue eyes—bluer than the ocean under a blazing summer sun. But their greatest jest bestowed upon me was when I was born into this world and it was discovered that I was... part crow—yes, like the clever avian—with great wings of darkness attached to my shoulder blades and large black talons in place of human feet.

So, you can imagine my tale growing up as a half-crow child who preferred to converse with the trees rather than learn how to swing a sword or hunt the animals of the land. My childhood was not easy, but neither was it difficult. The men and women dared not treat me ill for fear of my mother's wrath and later on, Jak's protectiveness. But I was never petted with warmth by the elders like the other children who ran amok. I never experienced unkindness from them, but neither did I receive love or affection from any of the *pias* or *pras* of the clan. Instead, there were many glances of wariness and thin-lipped smiles.

Your pardon, that is not entirely correct. There was one particular elder, *Pia* Yala, who formed a type of familial relationship with me. But it was many years of scoldings and childish disgruntlement before we formed the bond we share today.

Pia Yala had lived with our people since before even the birth of my mother's mother's mother, perhaps even much before then. She was practically an ancient with her long silver hair and disconcerting milk-white eyes. And being the eldest in the village had earned her the right to be as strange and crabby as she desired. Most everyone avoided her because she was meaner than the sting of a bee, and would often shout nonsensical things during the darkest part of the night.

Despite this alarming behavior, on the cusp of my fifth summer, my mother made it my duty to sweep *Pia* Yala's courtyard every morn. And I was to replace the cushion of the rickety stool outside her door whenever it began to fray. It soon became a habit for me to rise just after dawn in the hopes that I may finish my chore before the elder awoke because— although I felt a strange draw to her... *Pia* Yala frightened me with her uncannily perceptive eyes, and her strange ravings in the darkness when everyone was abed.

On a day when the summer sun was weak and the winds had begun to carry a chill, I became fed up with the grouchy elder after she had scolded and frightened away my favorite village puppy. I stomped my little bird feet into our home which always smelled of honey with the intention of taking the stinky-fish meant for today's meal and shoving it under a particular cushion.

But my revenge was thwarted when I found my mother seated at the table with her weapons neatly laid out and said fish already simmering in a pot of soup. I approached my mother and grumpily asked, "Why is *Pia* Yala so angry? If she is unhappy here, then why does she not return to her people?"

My mother paused in the cleaning of her favorite dagger. Her eyes were sharp as she replied, "Did *Pia* say something unkind?"

"No. I mean— yes, but not to me in particular."

The scraping and honing of her blade resumed and continued for many moments before my *Lai* spoke again. "*Pia* Yala has lamented many times that she can no longer return to her homeland. She relinquished that right when she agreed to become lifemate to *Pra* Olc."

My head tilted in a bird-like fashion as my child's mind digested this information. "*Pra* Olc... but-but- that was six generations ago! She is so **old!** How is she not dead?!"

My *Lai* snickered softly, then set down her work. She pulled me into an embrace that immediately banished my ill temper, and then she attempted to swipe back the hank of hair that always curled down my forehead over my right eye, but it stubbornly bounced right back into its place. "Yes, *Pia* is very old. She is... not an ordinary person, and she is to be respected above all others."

"But she throws sticks at the dogs! And she shouts at us when we run too fast!"

"Even so."

"But *Lai!* Just the other night she cried to the skies about a sacrifice! She is even more odd than myself! If she cannot return home, then why not move her further from the village? Where she would not be bothered by the dogs, or the running. And we need not be awoken in the night to her awful wailings."

My mother looked upon me sternly until I squirmed in my place. After five wingbeats, I lowered my head in shame and mumbled a prayer of forgiveness to *Pia* and the ancestors for my thoughtless words.

She lifted my chin until our gazes met and held me there. "Listen well, my son. Yala aht Te'rola may seem to be a grumpy loon that spouts nonsense to the night sky, but she was once more powerful than all of the clans on the island *combined*."

My eyes widened in astonishment at her words.

Nodding, she continued, "Oh yes, little bird. And she may still be the most powerful being in this land. She is not just a *pia* of our clan, she is **the** *Pia* over all the peoples on our green island. This is why strangers often travel through our village to pay their respects, and to bring offerings to the oldest Mother of mothers.

"But alas, with such a long life and so many people lost to the wars from before, the knowledge of her identity and her great service was not passed down in each family. And so, it is not remembered that she is due a holy reverence. Few remain that know of her significance: the elders here and further, some of the original surviving families, myself, and now... you, my little bird."

"What power does she have?"

"She is a Dreamer, the greatest one in an age. She has seen further into dreams than we can fathom. Many great calamities have been avoided, and our island has remained free of invaders because of her so-called 'wailings'."

My face flushes hot with shame.

"Her words are a wisdom beyond the realms and when she speaks of her visions, you must listen carefully. And, if you are ever asked to perform a task, you **must** give everything to help the *Pia*. Because the fate of our peoples may depend upon it."

There was silence for many moments as I reflected on the significance of everything I had just learned. "*Lai?*"

"Yes, little bird?"

"I will do as you say, but what about when she throws things at the dogs?"

She smiled warmly and kissed my forehead. "You tell *Pia* to stop fussing at the dogs and the children. But be mindful of your words to an elder, you may still honor and respect someone without allowing them to disrespect others. Understand?"

"Yes... I think I do. Can I ask for something, *Lai*?"

"If it is within my ability, then it is yours, little bird."

"May I have a bowl of soup and some honey bread to take to *Pia Yala*?"

She smiled broadly, "Of course you may. I will pack a small pot, and an entire loaf into a wooden basket to keep them warm for the journey. But, little bird, what will you do if she shouts at you like a surly donkey?"

It was several wingbeats before I gave my answer. "Then... I will loudly proclaim that she might be less grumpy if she ate some of my mother's delicious honey bread."

My *Lai's* dark eyes sparkled as she said, "I will wrap two loaves then."

We laughed joyously together as we gathered an offering for the greatest Dreamer in an age.

2

Bargains, trades, and an offering

My peculiarity did not wane as I grew into a young man, with my wares becoming more eccentric as my life extended. In a world under a constant threat of war, I valued things of beauty and I often wandered our little green island in search of things that would set fire to my mind.

During one of these forages, I found a smooth, frost-green stone at the shoreline. The color alone made it unique but the strangest part was that it held the memory of a warm, spring rain. I spent all evening listening to the ocean's sighs as I wrapped this extraordinary rock with thin wires of gold that I had gathered from the nest of a fire phoenix, and shaped it until it became a curling, delicate trinket—lighter than a feather and fit for a queen.

I was a fool to not have guarded myself better, and I lost that particular treasure not long after.

As I admire my newly crafted bijou under the light of the setting sun, a strangeness comes over me. My elation over my accomplishment swelling beyond my natural state until I become heady as if I have stolen into the wine stores. A part of me finds this a bit alarming, but I quickly lose the ability to comprehend the situation.

A faint humming begins to rise out of the darkening waters before me. It is a sound of such divine beauty that I begin to weep despite the panic within me fighting the haze that is invading my mind. My body feels as if wrapped in the finest of silks, and it gives no resistance when there is a compulsion to *relax*—obeying the command without even consulting the owner of said body!

There I sit with legs crossed in the sand, arms at my sides, clutching the stone wrapped in gold in my right hand, while staring numbly towards the dark water as the full moon rises higher into the sky. And I wait.

She emerges after ten wingbeats. At first, her entrance into our plane is a feigned coyness when her head breaches the water with a song caught on her cerulean lips like spilled nectar on a flower, but I see the satisfied flash of pointed teeth to find me in such a helpless state. I have no hope at all to escape now that her calling is no longer muffled, and she weaves a spell of compulsion so strong that the very air vibrates in obeisance as I am bound by an invisible rope, then dragged into the deep ocean.

I am surrounded by blackness for a time with only a luminescent tail-fin faintly glowing in front of me. I do not know for how long I float through the waters pulled by a siren to my death. At least she has the courtesy to spell me from drowning before we reach her lair—how thoughtful.

At last, we arrive to my tomb that is surprisingly well lit by bright moonstones lining the upper reaches, enabling me to have a proper view of my captor. Her skin shimmers between varying shades of cobalt and slate-gray under the light. She is a creature born of the deep and her coloring matches her world. Except for a shocking frizz of bright hair—it is the sunset before a morning storm—a flaming mix of red and pink with shades of gold. Despite myself, I admire the beauty of my captor—I suppose there are uglier ways to die.

She turns a depth-less black gaze my way causing a shiver to run down my spine, and she swims over to circle me while humming her song under her breath—releasing my mind from the haze but my arms are still bound. I quickly hide my newly crafted hair trinket in my palm, wondering if the gold might be hard enough to cause enough damage to her eyes; I doubt it very much with the softness of the metal. But there is no need to worry because the moment she opens her mouth to speak, my perception of her changes.

Her eyes shine as she exclaims, "You have wings! I have heard of your kind! How came you to be so far from your people, little crow creature? We used to have wings too, until my ancestors lost to the muses. I adamantly believe they cheated. I mean, how could *they* defeat *us* in singing? We are born with a song on our lips! But that was eons ago and my nursemaid Ipori says there is naught to be done about it in all this time but I think..."

I am momentarily mute as her glamour drops. Gone is the frightening demeanor of a powerful siren, in its place is her true self, a young girl hardly older than myself with frizzy hair that she continuously brushes out of her face while she chatters excitedly at me, her words stumbling over each other as they race out of her mouth.

After many moments, she finally stops and tilts her head in confusion. "Why do you not speak? My song no longer holds you."

My voice is quiet, "I was born on this plane, I have never known others of my kind."

Her black eyes soften, "Oh. How sad. But, at least you are special here! Being the only Crowkind amongst the Bound must be exciting. Do they revere you up there?"

"No. I am too strange for them, and so... I often find myself...excluded."

She spits indignantly, "Pah! Humans! They do not know how blessed they are! Do you fly above and taunt them? I certainly could not help myself if I were you. I would leap onto the backs of the winds and shout with joy to remind them that they are tethered to the dirt while I am free to dance with the winds. You must do this!" She pops a hand over her mouth, "Oh! Well, I suppose you cannot do that now since I am to feast upon you."

"Oh? Is that still the plan?"

"Why yes! I used almost all my power today and I certainly will not release you now. I did not think I could spell you at first, but you were so distracted that I just managed it. And I have been practicing with my nursemaid for many days before this. You are my first successful captive from above, and a fine one at that!

"Oh, I do hope I absorb your eye color! My Ipori says that most of us lost that ability long ago, but I am sure this time will be different. They are such a pretty blue and would match me well, do you not think? My dark-eyed sisters will be so envious if I return with eyes bright as the Surface." She giggles with her gaze far-seeing before spinning back to me with a slight pout. "It will be such a shame that your wings will never fly again, but I promise to keep the feathers in a place of honor in my lair. How does that sound?"

I clear my throat, "Thank you, I could not ask for better. But... might I attempt to bargain for my life first?"

Tapping her lips thoughtfully, "Mmm. I suppose I can listen to your offer. But it must be a very good one, else you will disappoint me."

"I promise it will be the best available to me at this time. Will you release my body so that I may have a few moments to myself?"

"Oh, very well. I grow tired of holding you in place, and it is not as if you could swim faster than me."

"Quite true."

She flicks her fingers and the invisible ties are gone, my body immediately sagging with relief. She brushes her hair out of her eyes and primly seats herself upon a bed of seaweed and soft coral. "I will give you a double dozen heartbeats before we continue. I am quite hungry and will become grumpy if you make me wait too long."

I bow my head then turn my back to the room. My mind racing as to what I could offer that would satisfy. Then I realize the answer is quite literally in my hand. "You wish to devour me for my eyes?"

"Yes. Your pretty eyes will look quite becoming on me if I can absorb the color."

"Did not your Ipori say that is unlikely to happen?"

"Well…yes, but I will not know unless I try."

"True. But what if I offer you something that will ensure you are the envy among your sisters? A treasure so unique, there is nothing of its likeness on either side of the Surface."

Her eyes are alight, "Show me."

I reveal the hair trinket on my palm. She flashes forward to view it, disappointment in her expression. "Although this is very beautiful, my sisters and I have baubles aplenty at the palace."

"Ah-ah. This is not an ordinary hair pin, this one contains a secret. Grasp the stone, Princess, and you will know."

Her delicately-webbed fingers wrap around the soft gold to touch the frost-green stone and she gasps. Her eyes look to me with wonder. "What magic is this?"

"I do not know how it came to be, but that is what I was occupied with when you "found" me. I was attempting to learn its power as I wrapped it."

The siren is only half listening, her eyes are closed as she relives the memory of a spring rain. Unexpectedly, a vision appears before me of her above the surface of the water, head turned towards the sky with the rain pattering softly onto her hair and skin. A soft smile crosses her face, she opens her eyes and looks to me. "I will take this wonderful treasure for my hair. My sisters will be too curious of the secret and I will refuse to tell them." She giggles as a mischievous smile curves her lips. "I also want two of your feathers since I will not be able to place your wings on my mantle."

My wings pinion back at the thought; I hesitate to give someone such an intimate part of myself, even if it is to save my life. I debate her demand for the space of a single wingbeat.

"With respect, Princess, I decline. This is akin to me asking for strands of your hair or for scales from your tail form."

"Ah. I see. I suppose that would be asking for too much." She pouts prettily, then opens her mouth to renege on the bargain.

I cut in, "But! I will offer you one flight over the waters on a day of your choosing. You may not have my feathers, but you can still appreciate their purpose."

Her eyes sparkle as she earnestly accepts, "Agreed!" She snatches the pin, then pulls back the left side of her frizzy hair, tucking and twisting her newly acquired trinket until it holds that half away from her face—the frost-green stone nestling beautifully among the sunset colors.

"I, H'roc the tinker, offer you a bijou crafted of phoenix gold with a stone containing a secret memory, as well as one dance with the winds in exchange for my life and to be brought to the surface unharmed. Is the trade satisfactory?"

Her sharp teeth flash at this last part. Bargains must be very specific. I do not believe she would have tricked me, but one can never be too careful.

"I, Princess Zai'lukar, heartily accept this trade to spare you and allow you to keep your pretty eyes. And in good faith, I will return you to whence you came in the same form that I found you."

BARGAINS, TRADES, AND AN OFFERING

* * *

As I begin my trek home tonight, it occurs to me that I will need to pass *Pia* Yala's hut, and I have not brought an offering since I have been trapped for hours in the waters. I think to skirt around it to avoid being stung, but I am exhausted and beginning to catch chill. Surely she will have retired at such an hour? I take the risk, fool that I am.

Pia is sitting on her worn, rickety stool outside the door, staring into the sky as she is wont to do, and she is whispering of strange things again. I soften my steps in the hope that I might sneak by while she is preoccupied, but it is not meant to be.

She abruptly stops her mutterings, and catches me at the edge of the moonlight. "You forgot my supper, boy."

I swallow my sigh as I turn with my hand placed over my heart and bow to an elder. "Forgive me, *Pia*. I was...detained and have not returned home since early morn."

Her nose wrinkles, "Is that why you are wet and smell of magic?"

Taken aback, I stutter my reply, "Y-yes. A siren caught me."

She harrumphs, but her milk-white eyes become sharp, "Their songs are a powerful draw and once in their domain, it is nigh impossible to escape. How is it that you stand here before me, wet pup? Whole and hale with all of your original parts?"

I smile sheepishly as I tell the tale of my capture and how I bargained with a sunset-haired siren for my release. *Pia* Yala listens intently with not a word uttered until it is finished. Then, comes a flurry of questions and demands.

"How long have you had this affinity for the *other* creatures? Have you any more baubles that you created? Bring them to me at once, I wish to inspect them. What materials do you use and where have you found them? Are they earthly things or *other*?"

I open my mouth to plead exhaustion and hunger, but my mother's bidding echoes in my mind. Resigned, "I will do as you ask and return shortly with my collection of bijoux, *Pia*."

She leans back in her stool with an odd expression. "Bring some of your mother's honey bread, and I will make a trade with you."

Thus, began my unexpected apprenticeship with Yala aht Te'rola, the Great Dreamer. *Pia* had decided that a half-grown, part-crow boy was worthy of her ancient wisdom. She opened an entirely new world to me, teaching me things beyond my wildest imagination and I soaked up every drop she poured into my young mind. I learned how to strengthen my affinity with the otherness of the worlds, and I began to craft in a way that allowed me to imbue my creations with magic that gave them life and a purpose if needed. My treasures became things of unearthly wonder, and my reputation among the *others* spread like fire, leading to bargains and trades of items I would never have been able to access previously.

I did not realize until many years later that *Pia* had *dreamed*, and the passing of her secret knowledge was for a greater purpose beyond the crafting of magical jewelry; that there would come a time when my creations would be of immense importance in the generations to come.

"*Pia! Pia!*" In my haste, I knock over and shatter one of her favorite bowls. I wince at my clumsiness because I know she will sting me hard for that one.

She does not hurry herself into the room. "What is it, boy?"

BARGAINS, TRADES, AND AN OFFERING

Never mind that I am now of marriageable age, I will always be 'boy' to the Dreamer. I drop a hurried bow while discreetly moving my body to hide the broken mess on the floor, then I carefully set down a large conch shell filled to the brim with darkness on her table. "Look what I traded a brother whale for!"

Her milk-white eyes glance over the shell. She sniffs with annoyance, "You traded for saltwater?"

"Not just any saltwater, *Pia*. It is the blackest, coldest water he could find."

"Oh? And what did he receive in return?"

"He wished to be reminded of warmth when in the deepness of his home. So, I brought him a shaft of sunlight that had gone astray."

She nods approvingly at my trade causing me to grin with delight. She asks, "What will you do with this blackest of water?"

"I hope to make a pouch from it, something that will retain the coldness of the ocean. Then, I can begin collecting."

"Collect what, boy? Out with it all. Your excitement is wearing me thin."

"Stardust! A piece landed on my shoulder the other night during my flight to the dragons' lair to check on the hatchlings and pilfer any empty shells. I believed it was snow at first, but it began to glow brighter and grew hot until it burnt into nothingness, leaving behind a small mark of ash on my skin." My chattering continues with no notice of the deep silence in the room. "So, I wondered if a bag that is darker than night and cold like the heavens would prevent the stardust from burning out." I take a breath to begin a long-winded explanation of my elaborate plans, but stop when I finally notice the expression on my *Pia's* face.

It is the one that is kept secret from the world. It was only by chance that I had seen it as a boy when I had stolen into the dark of night to feed the one-eyed cat that had stubbornly made its home in *Pia's* courtyard. She had been gazing into the sky with a strange stillness when I happened upon her. I observed her in a secret silence for many moments before finally sneaking away, completely forgetting to feed the cat.

The expression on her face that night is the same now, it is one of deep longing edged with a bitter grief. I think to offer a consoling touch, but that is not *Pia's* way. I turn away to clean up the shattered bowl, pretending that I did not witness such a vulnerable moment.

I have just finished clearing my mess when *Pia* finally speaks. "You will need strands of moonlight to maintain the shape, boy. Come tonight with an offering for Mother Moon and we will ask for a gift of some of her hair."

3

A luminous thread

The moon is nearly full when my sisters and I see him for the first time, a half-crow man with wings as dark as a moonless night flying low above the earth while meticulously searching the ground for something. We observe him for many moments, curious as to what he is doing.

In the next instance, he lands gracefully to pick up something no bigger than the tip of his finger. Despite its size, the object brightly illuminates the area around his hand. It seems he is scavenging for dust from the heavens.

My sisters and I are amused by this crow-man that seeks out particles fallen from the night sky. Finding our dropped shine is no easy task because it burns up quickly outside its natural environment. But he is beyond tireless in his efforts, and we chatter quietly together as we watch him zip back and forth in the Beneath looking for the telltale starshine.

It soon becomes apparent that he must have hidden knowledge because he will oftentimes wait in the exact place for a stardust before it even passes through the barrier surrounding the earth. We are further astonished when we realize, that not only is he able to find such specks, but he is keeping the stardusts intact by storing them inside a little pouch that hangs from his wrist. My sisters and I begin to wonder to ourselves what other surprises might be in store with this strange crow-man from the Beneath.

He is the talk of the skies for many nights after his sudden appearance, but it is not long before the novelty wears off for the others, and they return their attention to the ocean and the interesting things taking place there. But I am endlessly fascinated by his mission. Every night, I watch him fly the skies and skim the earth to collect stardust in a pouch hardly bigger than a nightjar's egg—back and forth for days, high and low for weeks, until his bag became full before the new moon had begun. Then he disappeared for a time.

It is on the third night of scanning the land below when I realize I am searching for the little crow-man, I did not know how dull my nights were before he arrived. Tonight, I turn away with a small breath of disappointment. And it is not until many nights later when Mother Moon becomes half-hidden that I finally stop looking for him.

Mostly.

Our Mother is in deep slumber tonight as I gaze unseeing upon the dark Beneath. A black shape streaks past, catching my attention and waking me from my stupor. My heart flutters with secret hope and I hold my breath as I watch for further movement, silently reminding myself that it may be another owl hunting for their meal. My eyes scan back and forth for the black shape, but the Beneath is too dark without the moon's light and I cannot find it.

An idea strikes.

I glance around to see what my sisters are doing, finding them busy excitedly chattering about the increasing number of moonlight trysts between the sirens and the merfolk ever since a certain rebellious, frizzy-haired princess hosted a secret masquerade. The young sea-people think their gatherings are hidden from prying eyes, but they forget about the heavens—they always do—we see all that transpires in the Beneath at night.

I check twice more to ensure they are too preoccupied to notice what I plan. Satisfied that I will not be caught, I slowly drift lower and lower to the earth, stopping just before reaching the barrier. Then I shine a bit brighter, but only enough to illuminate a small area for fear of drawing the attention of the others.

The earth under me is cast in a soft light, creating large shadows and I look over everything within view. Disappointment begins to creep into my heart the longer I search without finding him. But then, there is a soft rustle of sound and I turn my gaze to the source with my heart in my throat. I hear the gentle flap of wings once more before it finally comes into view.

It is him! My crow-man is barely visible, still slightly hidden in the soft shadows at the edge of my light. He flies slowly, skirting my shine and unknowingly teasing me by doing so. I almost shout aloud my frustration, but that is all forgotten when he finally enters my field of illumination.

I gasp when my starshine runs across his ink-dark feathers, creating a beautiful ripple of silver against the black. I doubt that he can hear me with such a great distance between us, but something causes him to abruptly stop mid-glide and he pulls upright, wings fanning slowly to keep him aloft as he looks around.

I have only ever vaguely seen his dorsal side from afar—dark wings with dark hair. Now, I am close enough to see that he has a head of thick waves that curl loosely at the ends, causing me to wonder if it would feel soft like a cloud. Which, for some reason, leads me to imagine running my fingers through his tresses, starting from the roots and gliding down the length to wrap one of the curls around my finger.

This thought stirs something deep within my spirit, and it feels as if something unravels in my heart. The strange sensation lasts all of three breaths whereupon a single luminous thread floats out of my chest. Before I can even reach to touch it, the thread shoots down like lightning towards the crow-man. I watch in horror as it stretches for him while still very much attached to my heart, and I begin to panic about what might happen once it reaches him.

But the thick string cannot pass through the dome, smacking against it softly before it lays motionless on the surface after being thwarted. Before it can do anything else strange, I quickly reel it in and tuck it back into its previously hidden place.

When I look back to the Beneath, I lose all thought, and all my breath rushes out as I am met with the bluest gaze I have ever seen. The heavens seem to stop as we stare at one another for moments or hours—I do not know—and something profound passes between us. I do not yet understand what it is, I only know that I am forever changed.

Suddenly, his wings beat powerfully behind and he launches toward me. I know he will not come close to reaching me, his earthly body is not made for the lower heavens and there is still the barrier between here and there. But I drift lower with a foolish hope fluttering in my heart as he draws closer.

I snap to myself when I hear a twinkling voice call my name. I quickly smother my shine, plunging him into deep shadows, and then I yank myself further into the heavens—the Beneath returning to a moonless darkness—before I am discovered by my family. There is no punishment for wandering close to the Beneath. But... just imagining the giggles and whispers and coy glances of my many sisters if they were to discover me admiring a creature from Beneath is something I wish to avoid. I hurriedly join them in their spirited discussion on who they think will be the first of the sea-people to break tradition by life-bonding outside of their own—my sisters none the wiser of what has just transpired.

    I eventually drift back to my place in the sky and coax a thick cloud to cover me for the rest of the night. I wish to examine the events of tonight without the distraction of a blue gaze upon me. *What was that?* My heart drums in my chest, thrilled that he has returned but also anxious from nearly being found out by my sisters. I extract the strange thread tucked within my heart, feeling its warmth, and there is a slight pressure when I gently pull the string. It is my heart thread that is tied to my spirit and I must take care with it. Closer examination reveals that the thread is a bright red surrounded by a hazy luminescence. How strange that it reached for a creature that I do not even know the name of. But I cannot deny that this half-crow creature has had my attention from the moment I lay eyes on him, and a part of me very much wishes to know more of the winged man.

    My cheeks warm when thinking of his gaze upon me. That moment of connection felt as if he reached out to gently strum my heartstring, and a yearning surfaced to echo deep within my spirit. My heart flutters wildly as I remember the intensity of his eyes as he flew towards me. I press a hand to my chest, hoping to suppress the ache there.

    I unconsciously fiddle with the red string the rest of the night as I agonize over these newly discovered emotions. Exhausting myself by the time dawn approaches, having gone round and round with no idea of how to move forward. As the sun grasps the horizon, a great yawn overtakes me, and I stretch sleepily before tucking into bed. I begin to drift off into dreams, and my last thought is of searching for a set of blue eyes at moonrise.

4

An insurmountable distance

Have you ever ached for something with no rhyme or reason? This feeling burned me day and night. It was something wholly new and alien to me that, for a time, I was unsure of what it was. I could not comprehend it, nor could I sate it. Then one day, it dawned on me what might be the cause of this yearning. I do not know at what point it happened. Maybe it was gradual like a fog that rolls in the night, or perhaps it had been all at once like a burst of sunlight. But... I fell in love with a star, and I had no idea what could be done about it.

It was nearly a moon ago when I saw her. I had been searching for stardust during the new moon with little success, but it was when I flew into a peculiarly illuminated area that I found something wholly unexpected.

I do not know how to accurately describe it. It was a faint calling that caught me, much like the lure of a siren song, but this pulled to me in a way that was vaguely familiar. It felt like the caress of the wind between my feathers, or the hum of a forgotten lullaby in my bones. It was something that called deeply to everything within me: body and blood, heart and spirit. Whatever it was caught me in flight and I hung in the air, waiting for the call again but it stopped as suddenly as it had begun.

I hovered in place, searching for the source, but found only the stillness of the earth in slumber. A strange hollowness began to skim my heart, growing larger the longer the call went unanswered. I had nearly given up when there was the powerful urge to look up, and the creeping emptiness vanished when I found the source of what had called to me.

It was a star hanging low beyond the barrier, she was so close that I could almost see the curve of her cheek and the vague shape of a mouth. The most defined features were her eyes that gazed upon me with astonishment. We stared mesmerized with one another for the space of twenty wingbeats, and then a deep yearning flashed in her eyes of silver fire that punched straight into my chest, and they were my undoing. I found myself propelled forward before the thought had even formed, such was my desire to meet this star. But in the next moment, she pushed deeper into the heavens, taking her light and plunging me into darkness.

I became a night hunter. At first, I would come under the pretense of searching for stardust. But that did not last beyond three nights, because all I desired was to sit and admire her. She was ethereal, a star that hovered low on the horizon and east of the wind. She did not draw so near as that first night but always, she remained close.

I became emboldened with each night that I felt her gaze upon me; so I began to speak to her as if she were near, speaking of all manner of things. I told her of making honey bread with my *Lai*, of outshooting cousin Jak during hunts, and I even spoke of *Pia* Yala and her grouchy tomcat. I regaled her with tales of my mishaps in pursuit of my crafts, and I described the beauty of our island in the daylight—which gave me an idea that led to a trade.

    We continued in this manner for many nights, the moon waxing and waning while I attempted to woo a star despite the insurmountable distance between us.

5

Water and fire

Early one morn, I travel somewhere that was found during my explorations, a place of reverent convergence. I stand at the edge of a high cliff that overlooks the wide ocean. In the distance is a dark green forest growing atop a great mountain. Pale gold streaks over everything before me, the sun's arrival awakening the creatures of the day.

I whistle a tune into the winds as they stream past me, the sound is immediately lost in their gusts. I am on my third song with still no response when I change tactics and I begin humming, then singing songs that I have heard around the communal fires. The sun climbs high into the sky, reaches its peak, then begins its descent to make way for the night.

There is foam at the corners of my mouth that has become dry as a desert and my lips are numb before I finally catch the attention of the winds. They all stop as one, and the air becomes eerily still. My ears throb with the sudden silence.

A Grandfather wind approaches. His voice is a rumbling gust, "You have lingered here a while? Or... perhaps not?"

I bow with hand to chest in greeting. My jaw aches and my voice cracks but I answer as loudly as I can, "Yes and no." Time runs strangely here.

"Why have you come to this place?"

"Strength to you, Grandfather wind. I am called H'roc of the Green Isle, and I have come because I wish to offer a trade."

His bushy brows unfurrow and he nods sagely. "Ah. You are the craftsman of which they speak. Tell us, Crowman H'roc of the Green Isle, what is it that you wish from us, the Great Winds?"

"Oh, mighty ones! I wish to send a gift to the heavens—to a star that hangs low on the horizon and east of the wind."

He grumbles softly in thought as he strokes his long, white beard. "That is a strange request, and would be easily done except we are quite busy with the movements of the world."

My face drops and I become quiet. I did not think of what I would do if I could not have my request fulfilled.

A soft rumble, "But..." Hope rises in me as the grandfather turns to his very large family. "Perhaps... a young one who has no great task to perform. Who among you will take this on?"

A great wave of sound rises up before a small, breezy voice emerges and a little wind comes forward. "I will assist in your quest. But what will you give me in return, Crowman?"

The rest of the gathering return to their tasks, and the sound of the winds grows into a howling roar once again.

I bow to the wind sister and remove from one of my many pockets, a tiny bottle carved from an opaque, winter-blue stone shot through with veins of silver. Holding it high, "I have three sips of rain that dripped off the leaves of a Memory Keeper from the Greenwood. I am sure there is much to be learned from the water."

She pushes closer before speaking, "That is a prize indeed for others, but not for me. I was formed in the Greenwood, and the Great Guardians have long shared their knowledge with me since I was in the cradle. This treasure is not a rarity for one such as I, unhindered to blow through all the realms."

I lick my dry lips but there is no relief since my tongue is just as dry. My brow scrunches with concern as I search my pockets for something that I could offer to this free-spirited wind that they have not touched themselves.

A tricky idea forms.

"Little wind Sister, I will return two days hence just after sunrise, will you meet me once again?"

"Hmmm. That might be a long while from now. Or, perhaps not. Will it be worth the wait?"

"I believe so. Please meet me again. I will bring you a great and rare treasure."

"A'right. I will come again. Do not disappoint, little Crowman."

"Until then, wind Sister."

I lean forward until I drop off the side and there is suddenly nothing between my fragile mortal body and the turbulent waves slamming violently into the large boulders at the bottom of the cliff. I snap my wings out to catch the winds, stopping my fast descent to an unpleasant death, and glide over the water towards a certain place at the edge of the shore where I hope to find a frizzy-haired siren.

"You dare to request such a thing from me, tinker!? Although we are friends these many years past, this is audacious even for you!"

"Please, Zai-"

Her black eyes bore into me. "It is *Princess* to such as *you*, mortal!"

Oh. She must be really angry to demand that I address her formally. I shrink back, "I beg forgiveness, Princess Zai'lukar." I tug nervously on the curl over my right eye before continuing. "Your Highness, I do not request this of you lightly. It is for something of great import to my he- to me."

Her eyes soften, but only a little. Her cerulean lips are curled tightly as she speaks, "Tell me what has clouded your silly little head so much."

We stare at one another and five wingbeats pass in silence. Then ten. She glares hotly at me, still waiting for my answer. I sigh in resignation.

My cheeks burn as I finally reply, "It is love, Princess. I have found the one that calls to me."

She gasps and all the anger drops away. She swims to the shore before climbing out on transformed legs—not quite human but close enough to pass from afar. The princess kneels before me in the sand, eyes bright with wonder but there is also a tinge of envy ringing them. "You have found your mate?"

My face flushes even hotter and I nod my head shyly. "Yes, but–"

She bruises my arm in her grip as she exclaims, "That is wonderful news, my friend! Tell me, what is she like? How did you find her? You must let me meet her! Oh! Will you marry soon?" She straightens regally, "I will of course grace your ceremony with my royal presence." Her body vibrates with excitement. "Oh, my sisters will be spitting ink when they hear that I am invited to a Surface celebration!"

The sand beside us is suddenly extremely fascinating as I run my fingers through it before I quietly answer—one sentence to stop all of her questions. "She is a star beyond the barrier."

She slumps and releases my arm before moving to sit next to me. Princess Zai'lukar is quiet for many moments as she gazes out towards the water. "Well, now. That is a conundrum, isn't it?"

I clear my throat. "Yes, it is." Brushing the sand off my hands before looking to the horizon where the sun slowly drifts towards slumber. "I hope to at least try. I mean to bargain, but I need something that the winds have never touched."

The siren sighs into arms braced over her knees. "While I feel your pain having found a love that seems impossible..." My head tilts and I look at her curiously, but she waves away my questions. "I will not grant you a scale from my fin."

I nod defeatedly.

"However, I offer you this."

She opens my palm and places a soft object into it. I hold the orb before me, the inside swirls with liquid fire. "Is this... lava?"

"Yes, from the deepest volcano in my kingdom when it erupted a lifetime ago."

Strong magic must have been used to be able to encase liquid fire within deep water like this.

"Oh, Zai. Are you sure?"

The princess punches my arm. "You idiot. You hesitate over some lava, but not over a piece of my body?"

I rub another growing bruise. "I am truly sorry that I asked. It was beyond unreasonable of me."

She waves my apology away. "I forgive you. I am sure you were temporarily insane, and your mind was clouded with desperate love when you made such an offensive request."

My cheeks darken as I sheepishly nod in agreement. Sighing, I push back the curl away from my right eye only for it to stubbornly spring back into place. "Yes, I sometimes do feel as if I am half mad."

"Better to be half mad in love, than half mad in loneliness."

"Perhaps. We shall see how this ends."

She spins to me. "So, tinker. I, Zai'lukar, Siren Princess of the Western Kingdom, offer you this rarest of treasures from the deepest parts of my lands, an orb of black water and liquid fire, in exchange for your magic tree rain..." A sly smile. "...and one favor in the future. Is this trade satisfactory?"

My body stills at this last part. I stare into her gleaming, black eyes. An unknown favor can be a dangerous thing. She stares back, haughty and triumphant. She knows I will not refuse.

My head is heavy but my heart is light as I nod, "I, H'roc the tinker, proclaim the trade is satisfactory and accept this bargain."

6

Wings of darkness

When my sisters were not looking, I would shine just a little brighter to see my light shimmer on the back of his ink-dark wings, sometimes catching glimmers of iridescence when it was bright enough. How beautiful they looked with my light running their length. I hid this from my sisters but the Moon knew. She saw everything, and she only watched in silence. I did not know if she would tell, or what she thought of my secret.

I did not dare approach the barrier again, but I watched him for many nights from my place in the heavens. And I strongly suspect that he knew, because he would often look up to smile sweetly in my direction, sending a curl of warmth to my heart.

It was not long before he began to lie in the field below my place and speak to me of his life and of the things that occurred in the Beneath.

Always, I listened intently, laughing quietly at his stories and marveling at the things he crafted. I often wished to reply, but my sisters were growing bored waiting for one of the sea-people to break tradition, and they would soon look for new entertainment.

He visited every night without fail. When the weather was fair he would lie atop the tall green grass and speak to me until Mother Moon set. When the weather was dreary with rain, he would shelter under a nearby forest of trees waiting for the clouds to disperse so that we might catch a glimpse of one another. In my heart of hearts, I knew that we could not be together but I ignored it. I wanted what I could have of him while it lasted.

How very naive of both of us.

On a cloudy night when the sky hums with activity, a young wind passes through the barrier. It stops halfway between the dome and my place—the winds can only reach so far before the heavens overtake their breath—and beckons towards me.

I drift over curiously, "Strength to you, little one. Why have you blown so high?"

"Bright light to you, star sister. I am tasked with a mission from a creature of the Beneath."

My eyebrows raise.

"He has sent this with the hope that you might know his intentions."

She stretches up, and I lower myself until I grasp the small bundle. It is a fiery-red autumn leaf wrapped around something. The little wind breezes forward to watch as I carefully unwrap it; both of us gasp softly when a tiny shard of rainbow is revealed, the colors still bright and vibrant despite the lack of sunlight.

Her voice is a little squeal, "Oh my! What a splendid gift!"

My smile is so wide, my face might crack from the delight of receiving such a treasure. We watch as the rainbow slowly fades in my palm until all that is left is the beautiful oak leaf. There is no need to ask of the giver, who else would send such a wondrous gift of sun and water but my tinker?

She says excitedly, "That singing crow-man indeed did not disappoint! Do you have a message in return? 'Tis part of our bargain."

"Oh. Umm... Please tell him..." My mind is suddenly blank. How does one respond to such a thing? And these will be my first words to him as well. I bite my bottom lip as I contemplate the perfect reply.

Out of the corner of my eye, I see one of my sisters approaching so I blurt out, "Thank you for such a lovely gift!"

She tilts her head, "That is all?"

I nod hurriedly, restraining myself from shooing her away as my sister draws closer. "Yes! That is all!"

With an impish smile and a wave, she blusters back down to the Beneath to deliver my lackluster reply.

My shoulders sag with relief and regret as I watch her cross into lower heaven.

Sister Eyah arrives, looking past me to see the tail end of the wind as she swirls down towards the trees. "How odd for it to come this far."

I quickly tuck the leaf into the sleeve of my gown. Keeping my voice calm and a bit bored, "Just a curious young one with too many questions."

She smiles in amusement. "Ah. Then it is good that I arrived too late. Those winds are such noisy creatures; I sometimes get a headache listening to them bluster about down there. I am surprised you were able to send it away so quickly."

I shrug nonchalantly before drifting back to my place in the sky with Eyah excitedly speaking of the latest developments between the sirens and merfolk. I nod and gasp at all the right times as she chatters for the rest of the night, but my mind is occupied with thoughts of a sweet smile and mesmerizing blue eyes.

* * *

We continued in this manner for a time, my crow-man sending secret messages and gifts by way of the little wind. My sisters were mildly curious about my visitor, but not enough to approach for fear that they too would be bombarded with endless questions. Besides, they were occupied with the unexpected turn of events involving the frizzy-haired siren and a mortal man from the Beneath. Nothing has happened as yet, but all eyes (except mine) were turned to the ocean's shore. And so, I was free to enjoy my courtship during their preoccupations.

Every night, I looked forward to listening to my crow-man as he softly spoke to me of the things of his world. Oh, how I wished to converse with him, but I did not dare with so many ears around me. He seemed to understand my desire to remain silent, and did not press me for a response. I very much cherished our one-sided conversations, but his gifts spoke to me in a way that he could not reach with his words. There was the time he sent a spill of rain with a beam of sunlight trapped within, and I was encouraged to drink it, leaving a pleasant warmth in my belly for the rest of the cold night. His gifts were usually things of daylight, something that a celestial being of the night sky such as myself would not be able to experience otherwise; they were treasures of such profound thoughtfulness and my heart swelled with each one.

All of the heavens is relaxed tonight because of a massive gathering of storm clouds that are too thick and entirely too slow, obscuring the view of my crow-man, and the heavy rains are preventing me from hearing him. Great storms such as these are usually welcomed by the stars because it allows us to wander away from our places without the Beneath noticing. But I am not at all pleased with this one, and I am becoming increasingly morose as the night lengthens.

I am quite surprised and beyond delighted when the little wind sister arrives—drenched and a bit peeved while muttering about the worth of her new ring. She passes over a bundle and swirls away before I can thank her.

This one is encased in spider silk with droplets of water clinging to the strands like jewels, and I am speechless for many moments after I unwrap it. I almost dare not touch it for fear that it might disappear. I finally lift it away from the silken strands and hold it up to admire under the light of the moon. It is a single ink-dark feather, crossing the length of my palm to the tip of my middle finger. I touch it to my face drawing the edge of it along my jawline, its softness caressing my skin in a way that lights a fire in my mind and parts of my body flushes hotly. An unexpected second gift releases, and I receive a memory of the winds gliding through his wings as he soars under the heat of the sun. I am at once delighted and envious, for I desire so much to run my fingers through his feathers and to feel the heat of the sun radiating off his skin for myself.

I am quiet the remainder of the night, then rushing away before the moon has skimmed the horizon. As I curl in bed, I tuck his feather under my cheek in the hopes that I might dream of sprouting wings and flying a great distance to the Beneath to meet my crow-man. A thought surfaces just before I drop into the abyss of unconsciousness, causing me to sigh sleepily with contentment but also resignation—I am in love.

7

Confessions of madness

My love for her is the sweet fragrance of a flower's first bloom, it is fresh and oh so delicate. My heart jumps with joy as I gaze upon her in the night sky and I suddenly feel as if the world is not large enough for everything that I carry within me. It is brighter than the sun, deeper than the heavens, and bigger than the blessed moon. If I did not already have wings, this feeling would gift me with flight so that I might feel the cold winds against my skin and the breathless wonder of an entire world beneath me as I soar through the deep blue.

My chest vibrates with effort as I contain myself. Even I am afraid of the strength of my feelings, and I do not wish to frighten my Star. But every unrestrained smile of delight, every burning gaze of yearning, and every soft sigh of suppressed longing between us brings another wave of madness, and my need for her swells to alarming heights. It is no longer just my heart that suffers, my body has awakened and it thrums with desires that I wish to express.

An entire moon cycle passes while I finish my latest project and I decide it is finally time to confess to the Star that hangs low on the horizon and east of the wind. My creation is crafted with things of my world, imbued with the magic of hers, wrapped with the essence of all of myself, and I folded in a secret memory that will release within her grasp. It is a gift for my Star, something that carries the message of what echoes in my heart.

My nerves are frayed as I call the little wind sister and request that she carry one last message to the high heavens. She agrees to this final mission and spins up and away from me before I can think to change my mind.

My chest struggles for breath as I rapidly pace the shadowed earth. My hands push through my curls and tug on their ends as the night deepens. My mind is bombarded with too many thoughts, and I shove them violently away before I scream. Time crawls by, and the continuing silence that surrounds me is torture. I worry my bottom lip between my teeth until I nearly draw blood. In all of this, I dare not raise my head to look, because I am deeply afraid of her response. And... a dark part of me hopes that she never answers.

On a sleepy night when there is little activity in the Beneath, the young wind sister arrives with a gift, it is an otherwordly necklace. The chain is as thin as a breath of air, and the medallion glows with the faint luminescent that is only found in the heavens. I trace a finger along the surface and a flurry of experiences enter my mind: wet sand squishes between my toes, cool water runs along my dark skin, the warmth of the sun soaks into the coils of my hair, a fresh taste of rain on my tongue. I take it from the little wind and gently cradle it in my palm. More magic releases and his memory becomes mine: *the winds caress my feathers as I glide through the darkening sky to land in a field of green and gold, lush grass tickles my brown skin as I lay upon it, and love fills my chest until I can hardly breathe as I look into the dark heavens with my blue gaze on a star that hovers low on the horizon.*

    The memory fades and I return to myself. My eyes frantically search the shadowy lands until I find a dark form. His head remains lowered and his face is hidden, but I read his message in the frenzy of his steps, in the anxiety of his hands as he pulls on his dark curls, and I see the fear that expels with each tremulous breath. This creature from Beneath, a half-crow man with wings of darkness, is offering me, a star that lives beyond the barrier in the upper heavens, his whole heart.

    I quietly thank the little wind sister and tell her that she need not wait for my reply, that if there is one, I will send it on my own. She nods with understanding and waves wildly, whereupon I note that her ring is vaguely cat shaped and I could swear I hear faint yowls of protest from her rapid movement. She rushes away before I have the chance to inquire about her new treasure—no doubt it is something wondrous that she received from the tinker. And so, I am left alone with the necklace and a question that needs answered.

    I sit for a long time with my thoughts as I debate all the ways that this will not work. How can I possibly accept the heart of a creature from the Beneath? I should never have let it come this far. We reside in two different worlds and cannot cross into the other without immense bodily harm. This is an impossible thing and we cannot truly be together. Perhaps it is better to end things now.

But... my heart aches at the thought of living every night without his sweet smiles or without his warm gaze upon me. To no longer see my soft light run the length of his dark wings might be my undoing. I swallow past the tightness in my throat and tears swell in my eyes as my mind continues to wage a war with my heart.

My legs are stiff with cold as I sit in my place in a dark field beneath her. The little wind sister has yet to return. My heart sinks lower and lower as the moon travels further across the heavens. A shadow of sadness grows within me. I cannot return home until I speak to her. I take several bracing breaths before looking up, immediately finding her eyes upon me. My blue gaze meets her silver one and it is as if lightning strikes me when I see her tears; my breath freezes in my lungs and my heart stops. The moment stretches as my body struggles to choose whether it wishes to continue living, or to expire in this very moment. The world darkens.

My heart chooses to beat just a little longer when she drops lower and lower in the sky until she is nearly at the barrier—the closest she has been since that first night. In the back of my mind, I register the faces of the many stars that turn in curiosity to see what is taking place tonight.

Then the star beyond the barrier smiles tremulously as she slips my gift around her neck. Soft gasps and whispers rise up behind but her gaze remains steadfastly on mine as three specks of stardust fall, bright as diamonds, breaching the divide and traveling a great distance to me. I stretch out my hands and they land soft as snow into my cupped palms. Their coldness sinks deep into my skin, and there is a moment of breathless disbelief before color and sound returns to my life.

I shoot into the sky, as high as my wings can carry me while crowing my elation for all the realms to hear—she smiles shyly and giggles at my enthusiasm. I hover beneath her on the edge of lower heaven, my lungs filling with chilled air as I stare at her with vibrant joy in my heart while she looks upon me with eyes full of love. Oh, how my arms ache to embrace her in this moment. A dark part of me whispers that there is still a great distance between us, but I brush it off before the words take root. It does not matter to me. She has accepted my offered heart and for now, that is enough.

But I am a fool to believe that.

The air is stifling on a night when the moon is near dark and I cannot be still. My skin stretches tight, my blood is hot, and I feel as if I might burst at the seams with all that my body holds. I feel the question in her soft gaze as she watches me tread the earth; there is concern in the crease of her beautiful brow as I circle the skies for the third time, and worry edges her plump, delicate lips as I stew in silence.

During the deepest part of the night, I force myself to land and lie under her place in the sky. I gaze upon her luminous form as the yearning in my heart suddenly becomes maddening, and I wonder if my desires will drown me. I want nothing more than to have her in my presence, to feel the rise and fall of her chest as I hold her close. I tell her this, and more; whispering so that no others might hear of how my hands ache to touch her, that I wish to trace my fingers along the softness of her cheek and to press my lips to her bare shoulder. My mouth is dry and my palms are slick when I tell of how every part of me trembles with desire for her. And I confess of my desperate need to hear her gasp my name while I pay reverence to her body.

8

Matters of the heart

Life is wonderful for a time until the morning I return home to find my mother seated at the table with a pot of lukewarm green tea and two near-empty cups. My *lai* having a guest so early is not abnormal, but it is the disquiet in her face that alarms me.

"*Lai*, what is the matter?"

She looks up, having been so deep in thought that she had not realized I had returned home. She straightens and gestures for me to sit. "My son, there is something I wish to discuss."

I nervously seat myself on the other side—the thin cushion still slightly warm from its previous occupant.

Her dark gaze finds mine before she speaks, "Bani's mother visited this morn... She asks for an arrangement for her daughter."

The tension in my body releases like an arrow, and I chuckle dryly with relief. "I did not realize Bani cared for Jak. I am sure he-"

She cuts in, "The request is for you, H'roc. Bani desires a match with you."

My voice raises with incredulity, "Me!? But I- She has nev-" I lean back and take a steadying breath. "I do not understand, *Lai*. But it is no matter as I am sure you declined."

My mother shakes her head, "I did not agree, but neither did I decline. She invites us to supper for further discussion at a time of our choosing."

"No, *Lai*. I refuse."

"H'roc, at least meet with her first. Bani is a lovely woman and-"

I stand up, unintentionally towering over my mother, so I drop to my knees before her and grasp her hands. "*Lai*, I cannot bond with Bani or any other woman."

She blinks. "There is a son as well."

"No, that is not the issue. I have given my heart to another."

My mother's eyes light up, "Oh! That is marvelous news, H'roc! Why have you not brought this person to meet us?" She taps me lightly on the head in reprimand. "I have been worried these many moons thinking you were sleepless because you were lonely, but here you are already half bonded. You must let us meet this person."

I sit back on my heels and sigh, "That is part of the problem. I have not brought her to meet you because... well..." My face warms and I glance out the window. "Because I have yet to meet her myself."

My mother's brow furrows. "But...did you not just say you gave her your heart?"

"Yes, I offered it and she accepted. But we have yet to meet because she is... She is a star that lives beyond the barrier."

Her face falls at my words, "Oh, little bird."

I rush to reassure her, "Not to worry, *Lai*. I will find a way for us to be together."

Quietly, "H'roc, look at me."

Our gazes meet and she holds me there. "I am sorry, my son, but it cannot be."

I open my mouth to protest, but she holds up a hand to stop me.

Her voice is gentle, "Even if she could survive our environment, there is always the danger of ambitious humans and, gods forbid, there might come a day when you are not there to protect her. She will never be able to live peacefully on this plane. And, your body will not survive the heavens."

A hundred thoughts race through my mind, and I open my mouth twice to refute her words but nothing comes out. Tears well in my eyes as I acknowledge the truth, something I have refused to believe in all of this time: I do not have anything that will keep my love safe in this world. And my lungs will fail before I even pass through lower heaven, much less reach the barrier and beyond.

I drop my head and the tears run rampant down my face. My *lai* gently draws me into an embrace and holds me tight as I lament the loss of a love that has barely begun.

My love for the star is like a ghost that haunts me. It follows me as I go about my day: on the sparring grounds as I try to banish my frustrations with sweat and exertion, in my crafting room as I wildly throw myself into a new project, during supper with my *lai* and Jak as they attempt to converse with me while concern deepens in their brown eyes.

The worst is when I lie sleepless in bed while the world is dark and quiet, and I am alone with only my thoughts and heartbreak. What might she think as a second night passes without me there to speak of life in the sunlit world? Or to send gifts of magic and wonder? Or to sit in silent awe as our hearts commune across two realms? A shadow over my spirit grows, and I clutch my chest as a deep gnawing pain grips me. My breaths tremble out with difficulty and tears drip down my temples to soak into my curls. A thought surfaces and I realize it is true—I am dying, my spirit is withering and it will not be long before my body follows. But what can be done?

On the third evening, just before sunset, I return to the field beneath her place and leap to the skies—half mad with grief. If I must bid farewell to my Star, then I will fly as far as my body will allow to gaze upon her face as I shatter our hearts.

My wings carry me far from the green field and high over the treetops, above the dark blue ocean surrounding our little island, and higher still. I know that I will never reach the barrier, but I hope to at least reach the lower heavens, and perhaps tonight she will approach close enough that we may speak to one another and I will be able to hear her voice for the first, and the last time.

The air grows cold and thin, causing me to shiver in my clothes and my wings begin to slow from the effort to stay warm. I should have planned this better, but I was panicking and heartsick over what I must do. The gods laugh again at my expense—finding the one who calls to my soul only for her to be unreachable.

I stop and wait for nightfall just barely past the edge of lower heaven, beyond this point the icy air continues to thin the higher one travels, and there will not be enough to fill my lungs. Already, I find it difficult to stay aloft, my wings fanning stiffly as I rub my extremities to keep my blood circulating.

Just as the moon begins to rise, my Star appears in her place, a luminescent celestial body gently pulsing white and blue with an outline of gold against the darkening sky. I see the moment she turns to find me waiting for her, panic and confusion flashes in her eyes before morphing to concern.

Oh, how my heart swells to see her so close, and I forget all the things I plan to say. The thought of bonding with anyone other than my love sits like a boulder in my gut. I send a quick prayer to the gods and my ancestors, pleading that I can somehow be with my Star.

I throw all my strength into my wings, launching myself further into lower heaven with a beyond foolish hope that the gods will favor me for once and allow me to reach the one who calls so deeply to my spirit.

9

A cold voice

I have just awoken for the night and am greeting my sisters when one of them murmurs, "That strange crow-man has never come this high. What might he be looking for tonight?"

My heart leaps to my throat as I spin around, hoping that Eyah is mistaken. But there is he, hovering just past the edge of lower heaven below me. Twinkling voices rise behind me as thousands of my sisters turn their attention to him. Even though I revealed our courtship, we have kept our interactions distant to maintain some sense of privacy. So for him to be here tonight in such a manner... Panic curls in my belly at what this might mean.

I gasp when he bursts further into lower heaven, heading straight for the barrier. Fear clutches my throat as ice quickly forms on his wings and he struggles against the weight, but he clenches his jaw in stubborn determination and his eyes are alight with a feverish desperation as he climbs higher and higher.

I do not understand why he is doing this, but I must make him turn back before it is too late. I drop to the barrier and shout in distress, "You must stop! It is too dangerous, my love!" Behind me, a thousand voices exclaim in surprise at my actions. I had forgotten about my family, but none of it matters anymore. All of my focus is on my crow-man. I gesture wildly for him to turn, pleading with my eyes for him to return to safety. This only spurs him further, his expression tells me he will not stop until he reaches me. But I know he never will.

His chest heaves uselessly as he struggles to draw enough air to fill his lungs. In turn, my breaths become urgent and deep as if I am trying to breathe for both of us. My heart stops the moment his ink-dark wings lose their strength as the twin blocks of ice attached to them begin to drag him back toward the Beneath. His blue eyes flash with fear, changing to resignation as he realizes he cannot fly anymore. He reaches out and looks to me with an apology, offering a bittersweet smile before his eyes roll back to show the whites as he loses consciousness, and then he begins to drop back to the earth—a flightless crow-man bound to smash into pieces upon landing.

I scream in horror and pound frantically on the barrier, tears streaming down my face as I beg for him to wake and fly! My voice becomes hoarse as I shout and plead desperately for him to be saved. I cry out to the heavens that I will give my life for his.

A cold voice says, "I will grant your heart's desire."

The barrier disappears under my hands and I drop into lower heaven. A thousand voices urge me to hurry! I throw all of my power into reaching him. If any creatures in the Beneath look to the sky, they will see a shooting star blazing towards the earth.

I hurtle towards him, both arms reaching and stretching, pushing to go faster. The earth appears to grow larger before us as we drop closer and closer. I use almost every bit of my power, and my body grants me a final burst of speed that is just enough. I snatch him into my arms at the exact moment that he leaves lower heaven, and with the very last of my power, I grow great wings of starlight limned in gold fire that flash out and cut through the air. I attempt to pull up, but the response is slow and jerky from my new wings because I do not know how to fly and this is not enough to carry us.

Terror grips me as we rocket through the sky at incredible speed. We pass the tops of the trees and I know we will meet the earth in a moment. I snap my wings closed around us and tuck his head under my chin. Tears well as I quickly kiss his hair that feels as soft as a newly formed cloud. I squeeze my eyes tight as I desperately cry out once more for the heavens to save my love.

10

All of the heavens

There is only darkness for a time, but something urgent calls to me. I wake to profound confusion, my mind struggling to place where I am and what has happened. I know only that my exhausted body is fiercely cold and my wings are encased in a thin layer of ice as they lay heavy beneath me. It is many moments before my eyes focus and I find the night sky above with thousands of stars pulsing strangely, and the moon burns brighter and colder than usual. My gaze automatically turns to a place low on the horizon and just east of the wind, a deep unease grasps my heart when I find only empty darkness there.

All the breath rushes out of me as memory returns and I painfully lurch to my seat, crying out, "My Star!" I search the sky in a frenzy, and panic chokes me when I cannot find her. A large shape in my lower periphery catches my attention and I finally look down. My heart stops when I see the dark form lying an arm's length from me. Crushed wings dimly limned in gold fire cover the body as it lays in a deathly stillness that grips my breath; I watch helplessly as their fire dies out and the great wings fade into nothing before my next breath.

Despair hovers close as I crawl over, my hand trembles violently as I reach out to my Star—I would know her in any form—and turn her to face me. A keening cry escapes me at the way her body moves like a ragged doll. I sob uncontrollably as I hurriedly gather her in my arms. My words are barely coherent as I pray to my ancestors, to the gods, to the heavens, and to anyone else who might hear my pleas and grant my greatest wish.

Unbeknownst to me, all of the heavens is listening, and every star above watches with bated breath over what is happening in the Beneath.

My heart stings with bitter irony that I can finally see my love up close. My Star is ethereal, her skin is as dark as the night sky, and her silver hair is soft, loose coils that halo her head, reminding me of a fully formed dandelion puff. I cup her frozen cheek, then lower myself to kiss her forehead, begging against her icy skin for her to open her eyes. A hundred wingbeats pass and still, she does not move. Desolation wraps around me and my cries echo into a world that slumbers peacefully, unaware of the anguish that grips me. I bathe her cold face with hot tears and it feels as if I might spend an eternity in this way. How can I go on in this world when the one who calls so deeply to my spirit no longer breathes? I will never again see her smiles of delight, or feel the press of her loving gaze, or commune with her in contented silence. The thought of a lifetime without my heart is unbearable.

As I grieve, snow begins to fall and a moonbeam appears to gently illuminate us. More and more flakes drop on us, beginning to cover every part of our bodies. I pay no mind to these things as I cradle my Star... until my skin begins to warm unexpectedly. I surface from my sorrow as I realize it is not snow, it is stardust falling from the heavens. A thousand-thousand specks glowing brighter and growing hotter until I feel as if we are encased in a sphere of fire.

It is difficult to draw breath in such heat and I wonder if I might expire from this strange phenomenon. The thought brings almost a gladness because then maybe I can be reunited with my love. But I cannot leave my mother in such a way. And, who will best cousin Jak during the hunts? Who will bring *Pia* Yala honey bread to soothe her tempers? I close my eyes in understanding that if I survive this, I am willing to continue on while carrying the heavy weight of my grief. It will be a listless life, but I hope that time will dull some of the anguish. A final three drops of tears fall to land on the face of my beloved.

It is an eternity later or perhaps not, when the heat and blinding light surrounding us vanish. My brows furrow in deep confusion to find that the thousand-thousand stardusts burned out but left me unharmed, although I am buried under a thick layer of grey ash. Everything inside me collapses when a tiny choked cough sounds from the direction of my lap. I dash away the ashes to uncover her face and she takes a small, shuddering breath—breathing glorious life back into both of our bodies. My cry of disbelief becomes incoherent sobs of hope as her chest begins to rise and fall in a steady rhythm. I lift her to sit up and hurriedly brush off the remnants of stardust. My eyes rove in wonder along her dark skin which is now dotted with silver specks of starshine, her body has become a reflection of the night sky itself.

I am still marveling over her faintly luminescent marks when my Star heaves a great breath, and I turn to find her silver gaze upon me. I am suddenly frozen with fear that this might be a dream. But then she raises her cold hand to gently cup my face and gifts me with the most radiant smile. A fierce joy overwhelms me as I pull her to me, my lips meeting her soft mouth and I kiss her with the fullness of my heart.

11

The touch of a mortal

His kiss is a myriad of emotions: fear, anguish, hope, joy, and overwhelming relief. But most of all, it is the kiss of someone who had believed their whole heart shattered. He breathes out the last of the desolation that had begun to suffocate him. His touch vibrates with elation as he caresses my face, his eyes shine with unbridled awe, and a laugh chokes out as tears stream down his cheeks.

There is a sharp pain in my heart as I imagine the torment he endured in those moments while I lay lifeless. And now it is my turn to weep, wetting the curve of his neck with my tears. We cling to each other tightly, consoling one another while also reveling in this miracle given to us from the heavens.

The position of the stars and moon has changed thrice when he begins to pull away, but I refuse to allow such a thing, hugging him as if I hope to merge our bodies. He returns my embrace, tucking my head under his chin, and his joyous laughter travels from his chest into my body causing the tightness around my heart to ease until it dissipates completely.

A soft urgency spreads as I nuzzle into his warmth, my breaths hot against his skin. The rhythm of his heart increases the moment my soft lips touch his throat, and I begin to trail kisses along the underside of his jaw. He swallows thickly and his touch is restrained as he rubs along my back and shoulders. He takes a deep breath and his exhale trembles when I reach his full lower lip. He lowers his head as I raise myself in his lap for our lips to meet.

This second kiss is a desperate need to prove to ourselves that we are indeed alive, and that we are thankful for the ability to touch, to taste, to savor each other. We have never needed words to express ourselves and there are no words needed now; our breaths are gasping and urgent, our touch is desire and frustration. Hands grip and explore, trying to eliminate this space between our bodies. When at last we break away, we press our foreheads together and take deep, full breaths to inhale each other's essence.

We are so enthralled with one another that we temporarily forget about the world around us. But we are given a rude awakening when our private meeting is interrupted by the presence of a single man stepping out of the forest to approach our nest in the field.

My love quickly lifts me to stand with him, then immediately steps forward and spreads his wings to block me from view. But I peek from behind to assess this intruder. He is of the same coloring as my crow-man but shorter in stature with a heavy build. I note the dagger sheathed at his side as he wraps a thin rope around his hands. My love tenses and I press my hand to the space on his back between his shoulder blades.

The stranger's teeth flash white and wide. He calls out, "What are you hiding, H'roc?"

"Nothing that concerns you, Ekir."

He creeps a bit closer. "Now, H'roc, you do not know that. The strangest thing happened earlier. I was on my way to set traps tonight when my attention was caught by a bright light streaking through the sky as it fell toward the earth, and it seemed whatever it was may have landed in this general area. I thought to myself that it might be a comet. Or even..." He pauses and smirks. "...a fallen star such as the one in the old tales." He stares at us in a hard silence before continuing. "So, I hurried myself from the other side of the forest to this place. Imagine my surprise to find you here with a pretty thing." He leans to the side, attempting to speak around H'roc. "Did you see the sky light up, sweetling?"

My love's reply is quick and terse, "We did not see such a thing. Perhaps you are mistaken. You certainly have come to the wrong place as there is nothing for you here."

The man clicks his tongue as he takes another step. "That would be a shame since I spent half the night traveling. But, it seems not completely in vain. Introduce me to the incredibly interesting woman behind you."

"No. I urge you to return to setting your traps, Ekir."

The man's face changes as he loses patience with this game. He flashes forward.

H'roc shoves me away just as the man tackles him to the ground.

I rush forward, meaning to help when a rope suddenly wraps around my neck and I am yanked back.

A voice rasps out, "Looks like Ekir was right. Seems we caught ourselves something interesting."

Too late I realize that a second man had snuck behind us.

I frantically paw at my neck, trying to release the rope but it tightens until I can barely draw breath, and then I am reeled backward like a fish on the line until I am an arm's length from my captor. I carefully turn to face this enemy. My eyes blaze and my dark skin begins to heat with my anger, the specks of starshine on my body pulsing brighter the angrier I become. His eyes widen in awe and he moves to touch my skin.

My voice is frost and fury, "YOU DARE!" I reach out to snatch his wrist before contact. Instantly, the man releases an ear-piercing scream, dropping the leash as he grabs his arm.

I am formed from the frozen darkness and burning light of the heavens, my touch is one that will burn to the bone any mortal body if I so wish it. Satisfaction curls in my chest as the man flails wildly and tries to escape my iron hold, all the while his shrieks of pain echo around us. I hold on for another heartbeat—marking him permanently—before I release his wrist. The man falls hard to the ground, wailing when he sees his ruined flesh; then scrambles away in terror, disappearing into the darkness of the trees.

I stalk over to where Ekir still wrestles with my love, somehow oblivious to what has happened to his partner. Rage courses through me to see him attacking my crow-man and I grab him by the back of the neck, burning him as I drag, then throw him aside. The man's scream is identical to the other's—horrific pain.

I help H'roc to his feet, checking over his body for any damage that was inflicted by that mealy-mouthed man, silently vowing to repay blood with blood. My love has too many dark bruises forming along his arms, neck, and face, and there is a small cut along his cheekbone. I spin back to Ekir with violent intentions, and his eyes grow white with terror.

But my love grabs my arm to stop me. Gasping, he says, "It is enough." He pulls me back to him—my burning rage dampens in his hold. He loosens and removes the rope from around my neck. His eyes are hard as he throws it to the ground. He spits out, "Leave."

Ekir cautiously stands, whimpering and grunting from pain.

My head snaps to him and he freezes. My voice rings dark and terrible, "You are blessed that my love is a man of peace, for I am not. I desire to **burn** you until your skin shrivels off your bones."

He looks to H'roc wondering if he might allow such a thing to happen, then he spins on his heel and launches himself in the direction his partner had taken.

I sag as the last of my fury dissipates.

H'roc expels a deep breath and runs his hand through his curls. "Well. That was… intense."

My voice is anxious, "My rage carried me too far. …Does that make you fear me?"

"A little."

My shoulders slump.

"But that only means I must remember to never infuriate you." He smiles gently and grasps my arms on either side, gazing at me with honest intensity. "And, perhaps I can worry a little less about your safety. In fact, maybe I will have you fight all my battles." He smirks, "I would love to see the look on cousin Jak's face if you throw him like you did Ekir."

I laugh in awkward relief.

He grins as he gathers me to him, finding that we are near the same height. "You were quite terrifying, my Star."

Adrenaline still courses through me. "He hurt you! And the other one dared try to touch me! I am a celestial being, my cold body is not meant to be touched by mortals."

"Uh-huh." His nose is buried in my hair and he inhales deeply. His exhale comes out as a whispered groan, immediately eliciting a heated reaction from my body. His voice is low and sensuous, "And what about this mortal? Will you permit me to touch you?"

I swallow thickly. My reply is tight with anticipation, "You are already doing so."

His eyes are dark pools with a fine edge of blue as he whispers, "Then allow me to explore your heavenly body further."

12

Entwined

Our third kiss is the release of many moons worth of long-held desire—full of breathless urgency and grasping touches. He pulls slightly away to catch his breath, our heaving exhalations mixing to heat the space between us. I give him two heartbeats before I sink my fingers into the soft curls at the back of his head and drag him back for our lips to touch again. Our tongues meet in a frenzied exchange of twisting exploration and the last of our restraint disintegrates in the inferno that is created.

We become lost in the language of our bodies, his deep groans reaching to stoke the fire in my belly while my soft whimpers caress the softest parts of his body. His lips slide along the curve of my neck, and he stretches the collar of my gown to expose my shoulder to continue his teasing trail. I suddenly become desperate for full and unrestrained contact, running my hands along his hard chest as I seek to remove his tunic but it is designed in such a way to accommodate his wings and I growl with frustration at my lack of success. I have just made up my mind to tear it to shreds but he grabs my hands to stop me; his laugh is low—the heat in my body consumes the sound—and he kisses my hands before pointing upwards.

My baser instincts abate enough for me to realize that we are still in the field, under the immense night sky with an unimpeded view of the entirety of the heavens. My face flushes to think that some of them may have been witness to my wanton urges thus far. Celestial beings are so far removed from the things of the Beneath that seeing the more intimate moments is viewed as the course of nature and not thought of as anything beyond that. I am sure that their gazes are currently averted, but I am not comfortable with such openness. We remove ourselves to the trees, finding a soft place under a thick canopy where there is just the right amount of illumination from the moon through the branches.

The fire in my belly swirls and curls as I watch him release the ties and buttons that hold his tunic in place. I eagerly reach to pull the shirt past his wings, accidentally glancing along their edges as I do so, eliciting a sharp intake of breath from him.

I snatch my hands away—suddenly unsure, "Was that too much? Did I hurt you somehow?"

His eyes are deep pools of darkness and his reply is hot, "Yes. And no. My wings have never felt such... intimacy."

Oh. I whisper, "Do you want...?"

His eyelids flutter briefly and a muscle ticks along his jaw. His voice is low and strained, "**Yes.** I beg for you to touch me again."

The heat in my belly drops to my core, then spreads to set me completely aflame. I tentatively reach out, this time purposely stroking the edges, watching his chest rise rapidly in response. I glide my fingers carefully through his feathers and his breath expels shakily. My touch is lingering and becomes more teasing when his hands clench into trembling fists. Finally, I run the pads of my fingers up to touch where they are attached to his shoulders, delicately swirling the skin there. He spins around and grabs my hand to yank me down, our noses almost touching. My eyes widen when I see the hot urgency there, and then he drags me in—our lips smashing together as my body drops into his burning embrace.

We become a frenzied, gasping tangle of urges and senses: kneading, licking, pressing, grinding, scratching, and nipping as we explore the depths of our desires. And, as promised, he pays an almost holy reverence to my body. Tasting parts of me that make me tremble uncontrollably in his hands, while his breaths burn against my skin as he whispers his adulation. My hands grip his dark hair, my hips arch into him, and my vision blurs from the immense pleasure as he worships me with a firm mouth, a glancing tongue, calloused hands, hard embraces, and gliding fingers—all this to coax my body towards divine release.

It is my turn to beg, breathlessly pleading and desperately squirming within his grasp until I feel as if I might explode from unfulfilled frustration. My voice vibrates with fervor when I demand that he give me all of himself. A damp curl falls over his right eye as he moves to obey, I swipe it back and bury my fingers in his soft hair just before he merges our bodies. I unexpectedly scream as I am raised to a new level of intensity. And then we morph into a dance of giving and taking, of whining whimpers, guttural groans, deep cries, and aching sounds as our bodies become a rhythm of desperate movement searching for release. My moans build in volume as his hips drive into me until I am swept over the edge, and he hungrily captures my cry of release with his mouth before gifting me with a drawn-out groan as he follows me off the cliff.

We lie in a dripping, sweating heap of bliss, our limbs wrapped around each other as we revel in the aftermath—bodies deliciously sated as our breaths slow until they match pace. A luminescent haze envelopes us as something strange begins. Both of us are unsure if we are still conscious as we watch in awe as our heartstrings emerge to meet before beginning to softly twine together, weaving an unbreakable pattern until there is a thick, luminescent red braid connecting our hearts, and joyous elation grips us upon its completion. We simultaneously release a deep sigh of sleepy contentment before tucking tighter into one another, drifting off into the abyss of dreams with our bodies and spirits entwined.

13

A fallen Star

The night is stretched thin and on the cusp of giving way to dawn when we come upon *Pia* Yala's hut and she turns her milk-white eyes towards us as we approach, waiting on her rickety stool with the old tomcat fast asleep between her feet. I bow to my elder, then turn to introduce my love, but I freeze when I see the expression on my Star's face. Her eyes are huge with astonishment before she drops into a kowtow. Her voice rings with awe as she proclaims, "It is my honor to meet the Star who fell from the heavens so that she may *dream* for the creatures in the Beneath."

Pia Yala bursts into creaking cackles in response, then reaches down to raise up my love. Despite the mirth lining her voice, *Pia's* eyes shine with wetness under the lamplight as she says, "Is that what is believed of me?"

The tears are gone when she turns to me, holding up a hand to stop the jumble of questions about to spill from my lips. "Close your mouth before you give me a headache. You will get your answers soon, as I have many things that need said. But first, you must fetch your *Lai* and cousin. The time has arrived and there is much to be done."

My brow furrows and I draw a breath filled with confusion but she hisses like she would to a disobedient puppy. "Boy. Do as I bid."

I close my mouth, grumbles lingering along the edges. I reach to grasp my Star's hand but *Pia* stays me. "No, no. Leave Elloi here. I must speak with her."

"Elloi?"

This time she swats me on the hand, leaving a stinging sensation. "You bonded without knowing her name?"

My face immediately heats and I shuffle my crowfeet under her sharp gaze. Five wingbeats pass, and still, she waits. *Oh.* She means for me to actually answer. I rub the back of my neck before mumbling sheepishly, "There were more…. pressing…"

"Ack! Never mind that." She grumbles but there is amusement in her tone, "…priorities of young love." She shoos me away, then beckons for my Elloi to help her up and they both turn to enter the hut.

I whisper my love's name to myself, grinning foolishly before I turn towards my home that smells of honey.

* * *

My mother is practically vibrating with glee after meeting my Star, barely containing her joy as she sits at the table beside Yala aht Te'rola, a star that fell from the heavens to live among mortals.

Cousin Jak is his usual solemn self as he greets Elloi as a brother would. He only looks mildly curious as her skin changes color before our eyes, fading from a deep black-violet to a gold-tinged soft blue as dawn arrives, and the blue becomes more vibrant as the day progresses—her celestial form reflecting the colors of the sky. Jak moves to serve steaming tea first to *Pia* and *Lai,* then fills our cups as well as his—as if pouring tea for a wondrous creature from another realm is not a rare occurrence for him.

The silence in the room grows as the tea is consumed and we wait for *Pia* to begin. Yala sets her new ceramic cup down, then tosses a piece of stinky-fish to the old one-eyed cat. Her eyes are unfocused for several moments before she finally turns to me. "I have *dreamed,* boy. In another age, a great evil spreads over all the lands, not just our green island. It will be a thousand generations until it is formed, and another thousand before it begins to wreak devastation, but there is no doubt that it will happen. I have *dreamed* it many times and always, it comes."

I lean forward in my seat, "What is there to be done, *Pia*?"

"A weapon of immense power must be forged. All of these years past have been spent passing my secret knowledge to you—a creature of two realms—in the hopes that you would master the skills needed to craft such a thing."

A hundred thoughts crowd my mind at this revelation, and so many things from before begin to make sense. I sit back as I review all the hints and signs over the years that told me this. But I had never believed that I would be of any importance beyond my small circle, and to suddenly have this immense task dropped on me... It is beyond overwhelming. My throat tightens making air difficult to pass through, and a darkness grows around me.

Elloi reaches over to grasp my hand tightly in hers. I pull back from the edge of panic to look into the eyes of my beloved. The strength of her faith gives me courage. I turn my gaze to the Dreamer whose eyes are soft with sympathy and regret. I nod firmly, "Tell me what I must do and it will be done."

Pride replaces the sadness in her eyes and she dips her head in return. "The essence of a star is needed for-"

I leap to my feet to stand in front of Elloi. Surprisingly, Jak is there beside me. *Pia* clicks her tongue in exasperation and waves us off. "Not her, boy. It will be me."

This is met with stunned silence for a single wingbeat before the room explodes in a chorus of protests and disbelief from all four of us.

She slams her hand onto the table, making my mother jump. "You will not override me!" She glares at each of us. "The heart of a star is the only thing that may be powerful enough to stand against the coming darkness. Unless you wish to give up your bride, H'roc, or you have the power of the heavens hidden in your cloak, Jak, the only option before us is myself."

My mother covers her mouth with both hands, while Jak blows out a loud breath and grips the dagger at his side. And Elloi sits in silence. Everyone reluctantly accepts her decision, but I will not. I kneel at her feet and grasp her hands—they suddenly seem so frail and small within mine. Tears well thick and hot in my eyes as I beg, "There must be another way. We can ask the *others* if they know of a power that can be obtained for this."

My *Pia* speaks with a gentleness that I did not know she possessed, "Boy. Look at me."

I stare into her milk-white eyes—noticing a faint silver around the pupils—and her gaze is firm. "Mother Moon spoke to me of these things long ago, that a great sacrifice would be needed. I wailed my despair at the time but there was naught that could change what is required. For many years I consulted with the heavens, waiting for the signs. I did not know when until you arrived in my courtyard with your Star."

A sob chokes out of me.

"Do not sorrow for me, boy. I have long grown weary of this world since my Olc left this plane. It was many lifetimes before I found something to crack my hardened heart. And now, the time draws near for me to finally end this mortal life. I will have much to say when I meet the gods."

Her smile is bittersweet when she says, "Tonight, when Mother Moon is full and her face is upon us, you and your beloved will bow thrice to honor the gods, to honor your family, and to honor your union. And all of the heavens will bear witness to your promise to one another."

She cups my cheek—she has never done such a thing before—and my tears spill. "Then, you will offer the ceremonial wine to your *Pia* and *Lai*, and we will all rejoice and celebrate for three nights. When the moon sets on the third night, you will take your Star to the field that overlooks the ocean, there you will find a half handful of stardust—make sure that every speck is placed inside your little pouch. And when the sun breaches the horizon, you will find a silver crystal the size of a dragon's egg. Elloi must be the one to retrieve this and keep it safe. You will use these things to imbue one of your creations with great power, then you must travel to a sacred place of convergence, and wait for the one who will come for the weapon born of a star."

14

Stinky-fish and honey bread

Cousin Jak helps drape my late father's marriage robe—my *Lai* had wept when she pulled it out of the trunk where it had been carefully stored long ago in anticipation of my future union—around my large wings, and secures the ties along the back and sides while I nervously fidget with the collar buttons. I smooth down the red silk, tracing along the embroidery that depicts a tribe of winged creatures soaring across my chest, and I marvel at the intricate details woven with thread that was spun from phoenix gold. Finally finished, Jak steps back.

I exhale a deep breath and look to my cousin who has been a fiercely protective brother to me over the years. "Does it suit?"

He scratches his newly-grown dark beard and his brow furrows as he inspects me in silence for many moments. "Turn to the side."

I shuffle my crow feet—we had to modify the slacks to ensure my talons would not shred the hem.

"Hmm. Spin the other way."

I nervously turn.

"Well, that is unfortunate. Hold out your arms, and bend down."

I comply with his request. "What? What? Did I ruin it?" I chatter nervously, "Perhaps *Lai* will have anoth—"

He chuckles, "Peace, H'roc. I jest!" He smirks, "You make a tolerable enough bridegroom."

I straighten and glare at my annoying cousin.

Jak bursts into laughter. It is another moment before I join him, and the last of my nervousness fades. He steps forward to straighten my collar and pull down the cuffs at my wrists. Then he drags me down for us to briefly touch foreheads. His voice is one of quiet joy when he says, "She is blessed to have one such as you."

He claps a hand on my shoulder. "Come, we must not keep your lovely bride waiting."

I grin like a lovesick fool, and we step outside just as the last of the sun's light dips below the horizon.

Jak is telling me of how quickly his warriors were able to capture Ekir and his man to be brought before the council when he suddenly stops mid-sentence; his eyes widening at something behind me. I spin around to find the gathered villagers also in stunned silence with all eyes turned toward the entrance of *Pia's* courtyard where an otherwordly figure stands at the threshold illuminated by the firelight.

The new arrival is a woman of devastating beauty with sunset hair braided, twisted, and pinned back in an attempt to tame the wild frizz away from her face. It is possible that the darkness of the evening makes it seem as if she possesses inhuman, pupil-less black orbs for eyes. And it can be said that the strange moonlight causes her skin to appear as if it shimmers in tones of slate and cobalt.

The torchlight does reveal that she is dressed in a flowing gown dyed in such a way as to create layers of color along the fabric; the top section has an edge of gold that glitters over a crystal-clear blue that demurely wraps her torso, darkening to a midnight blue along her hips and down the length of her thighs until it fades into a pure black from the knees down to the tiny fire pearls along the hem that hangs to perfectly cover bare feet that may or may not have delicately-webbed toes.

She anxiously searches among the people before her until she finds me and smiles in relief. She glances at the person beside me, eyes lighting up when she sees Jak. My cousin's demeanor changes when their gazes meet, it is as if he is frozen in disbelief and his eyes shine with an intensity of emotions that I have never seen from him.

I curiously look between the two for several wingbeats until I arrive at several revelations. I rush to greet my guest—leaving Jak to stand awkwardly by the altar.

"Princess Zai'lukar. It is an honor for you to grace my bonding ceremony with your presence." The moment I speak, the spell over everyone snaps and they return to their activities—although, a little less hurried as they curiously observe us.

Zai reaches for my hand, and I wince at her grip. "Oh!" she releases me immediately. "I am sorry! I am just beyond excited that I did not miss the offerings. I was convinced that I would arrive too late because I became lost! I had forgotten to ask for the location of your village and I was stumbling around in the forest for what seemed like ages! And I was shouting curses to the sky after I had tripped over yet another tree root—I do not understand how you Bound tolerate needing to *walk* everywhere, it is a tortuously slow method of travel compared to swimming or flying, if one has the wings for it, but I suppose..."

I chuckle at her ridiculous rush of words before guiding her back to the point, "How did you find your way, Zai?"

"Oh, yes, that. Well, a large cat suddenly appeared out of the dark and very loudly and very insistently yowled at me until I followed it and found the path that led me here." She suddenly points to the rickety stool. "There it is!" She calls over, "I forgive your rudeness since I have arrived in time." The old tomcat ignores her as it continues to groom its tail.

"I must reward him with a very fat fish later." I bow and motion her forward, "Come, come. I will find a place for you as my honored guest."

The moon has risen to her highest point, and a shaft of light beams down to gently illuminate my bride when she takes her first step onto the path with a line of well-wishers to either side. There is an awed hush as everyone feels the veil of magic that settles over the place. It is more than just moonlight shining on the bride with skin that illuminates from speckles of starshine. It is a palpable presence, as if the goddess herself has come down to bless our union.

My beloved possesses a beauty unlike any to be found in all the realms, and I have to remind myself to breathe as she approaches. Her dark skin is a beautiful contrast against the white ceremonial gown gifted to her from *Pia* Yala—the same one the Dreamer had worn when she became lifemate to *Pra* Olc. Since my bride is nearly as tall as myself, the hem falls a bit short to brush along the tops of her ankles, but no one is looking at her feet because all of their attention is focused on the celestial being crossing the courtyard in a gown that softly glows with magic from the heavens. Anytime my Star moves, the lamplight catches to run along the woven strands of silver making it seem as if hundreds of shooting stars are racing across the whisper-thin fabric.

I almost come undone when she stands before me, losing myself in her gaze of silver fire. My heart swells and tumbles with jubilation that she is my bride—her smile growing wide as she feels it through our heartstrings. Our bond goes beyond romantic love. We are of one mind with no words needed for the other to know what is unsaid. We are one spirit sharing all that passes within: my pain is her pain, her joy is my joy. I have found the one who calls to me so deeply.

I grasp her hand as we turn to kneel before the small altar, *Pia* seated to the left and my *Lai* on the right with the ceremonial wine still warm on the table between them. Jak approaches with a large bronze bowl and *Pia* dips a branch with the greenest leaves into the clear salt water, then flings cold droplets onto our bowed heads. She swirls the leaves in the bowl twice more, sprinkling the area around us as my mother begins the prayers of protection and blessings over us. Near the end of the ritual, we bow thrice under the heavens as so many others that came before us have done. We finish the ceremony by offering wine to the elders of my family, and then to each other. A great rejoicing sounds from those around us as we drink the wine—sealing our bond to one another.

The atmosphere is joyous as everyone feasts together. The sweet wine flows freely when the music begins with the elders clapping and smiling wistfully as they watch the young ones dance in a large circle, leaping and spinning and laughing as the night deepens.

Not far from my place, there is a familiar uproarious laugh—not delicate or demure in the least—that very much belongs to a frizzy-haired Princess. Jak leads a grinning Zai to join the festivities at the same moment that I draw my bride into the circle of bodies, gripping her hand tightly in mine as she attempts to learn the steps of my people. Everyone is kind and patient with her as they guide her through our sacred dances. And each time she shyly giggles at her mistakes, she endears herself further into the hearts of my clan.

* * *

Word spreads like fire across the island that the Great Dreamer's time on this plane is coming to an end. And by moon rise of the third night, there is a bevy of travelers from neighboring clans with gifts and blessings for us. But their main purpose is to bid farewell to the Mother of mothers.

Some time during a lull after the feasting and before the dances, an elder from another clan lumbers slowly to our table with the help of a curly-haired grandchild, and proclaims that he wishes to gift the newly bonded couple with an old tale that has passed through generations of his family. A well-worn stool is brought forth and he groans with effort as he moves to rest his weary bones. It is many moments of hushed expectation before he begins the story in a voice gravelly with age and wisdom.

Everyone listens in rapt silence as he speaks of a time long ago when there was great upheaval on our green island. His voice trembles as he tells of how the wails of widows and mothers echoed over the waters as the land darkened with countless wars against invaders.

"The desolation grew to such heights that the sounds of sorrow reached even the heavenly realm. The gods heard the cries of the people but they believed that naught could be done and so, the blood of too many clans continued to soak the soil and to spill into the surrounding the waters.

"Until one dark night when the Moon goddess awoke from a dream in the middle of her long slumber and witnessed the endless river of tears dripping down the faces of the mortals below. And she knew that the peoples of the little green island would soon cease to exist. She greatly pitied these fragile creatures of the Beneath. So she called upon the children of the heavens, her voice ringing with a coldness that seeps into the bones, "A sacrifice is needed. Who among you will give up your heavenly seat to save the humans?" A deep silence was the only answer she received.

"For three nights she gathered all of the heavens to her, and each time she asked this of them. It was on the third night that a small celestial being stepped forward and answered, "I will go, Mother." The goddess smiled and gestured for her daughter to draw near, and then she kissed the star's brow, bestowing upon her the power to dream beyond the realms. That night, every mortal that happened to be looking up saw a trail of white fire streak across the sky as a star fell from the heavens to live among the mortals.

"The fallen star became known as the Great Dreamer, and for a time, she was given the honor and respect owed to one that had given so much to creatures that had lived beneath her. But alas, eventually the ones who knew of her great sacrifice and service were called home to the gods, and it was a terrible oversight that they did not pass their knowledge to the ones left behind.

"Peace slowly came to the island, and in time, the memory of her works was all but forgotten by the clans except for a small few. The goddess wept cold tears to see this, and all of the heavens cursed the humans for not honoring their beloved sister. To this day, it is the greatest shame carried by our people."

There is a profound stillness over all of us as we slowly pull from the tale. The elder's face is wet with tears and he gestures for his grandchild to help him up. We watch as they shuffle over to where my *Pia* sits on her rickety stool with a recently replaced cushion. Tonight, her silver hair is loose down her back and shines under the moonlight. Her robe is one of smooth red silk trimmed with phoenix gold and dotted with rare gems. Her back is stiff and straight and her chin is lifted just so when the storytellers kneel before her.

The elder shouts in a great voice, "This humble mortal begs forgiveness from the Star that fell from the heavens for the suffering you have endured all these generations as you languished in this earthly realm. My children and their children and a thousand-thousand generations of my clan will speak of your great sacrifice and you will be honored by my bloodline, always." The man and his grandchild lift their arms in supplication and then kowtow until their foreheads rests upon the dark soil.

Immediately following suit, my mother, my Elloi, cousin Jak, and even the Princess press their brows into the soft ground. Then a great wave of movement occurs where the entirety of the courtyard drops to kowtow to the *Pia* over all the clans until I am the last one still kneeling. And so, I witness the change in my *Pia* as the grief and bitterness fall away until she blazes with a luminescent light—looking like a queen seated before the people of her kingdom. Her gaze meets mine, our eyes brimming with unshed tears. I cover my heart with my right hand and bow deeply before dropping into a kowtow to honor Yala aht Te'rola, the greatest dreamer in an age.

The night is deep and the moon drifts closer to the horizon as my family and I gather at the edge of the forest. A great weight lays over my heart and I find it difficult to draw breath as I watch *Pia* bid farewell to the others by touching foreheads briefly. She kisses the head of the one-eyed tomcat that is currently being held hostage by Jak who now sports an impressive number of bloody scratches on his cheek and forearms.

My chest shakes and my breaths hitch with suppressed tears when she finally reaches me. She pulls me down to press our brows together and for the space of five wingbeats, we breathe each other's essence. I desperately wish for the next moment to never come.

Her voice trembles ever so slightly, "Do not forget all that I have spoken, boy. Your Elloi must be the one to carry the crystal until it can be set in the weapon."

I nod stiffly.

"And make sure my cat is fed two fat stinky-fish a day."

A tear slips down and I quickly brush it away.

Her brow furrows, "I will allow you to grieve me for three days and three nights. When the sunlight touches the ocean on the fourth day, you must begin your work in earnest. It may or may not be a long wait for the one who can wield the power of the heavens. Make no mistake, this will be the hardest journey of your lives for you and your lifemate. I urge both of you to draw strength from one another, else neither of you will survive this."

"You truly believe that I can create what is needed to save our world?"

She harrumphs, "Pah! Of course I do. Why else would I endure your endless, headache-inducing questions all these years? You are my chosen heir, inheriting my home, my cat, and my secret knowledge. I have every confidence that you will not fail me."

My voice cracks, "Thank you, *Pia*. For- for all of it."

She nods and says, "The time approaches quickly, I must go."

A sob bursts out of me and I pull my *Pia* into my arms, breathing in her unique scent a final time. She returns my embrace for ten wingbeats before reluctantly pulling away.

She swallows thickly and her voice is tremulous, "Pass me the basket of honey bread, my boy."

The air is filled with sounds of muffled weeping as she journeys into the forest until she slowly disappears within its dark depths.

Suddenly, there is a very loud and indignant yowl, followed by a sharp hiss of pain as a furry ball of anger leaps out of Jak's grasp. It is only a moment or two before the old tomcat is also swallowed by the darkness of the trees as he chases after his servant, giver of stinky-fish, *Pia* Yala aht Te'rola, the Great Dreamer.

A Lingering Dream: The Celestial Sagas, Book one

Something lingers...
  A poison
  A spell
  A fugue
  A deep longing
  A dream

I thought nothing of it, the men that I would love in my sleep. They were just the desires of my heart made tangible in the dream world. But an idea grew into suspicion. Could one of them be real?

It became an obsession. He must be real. Why else would I wake with such pain in my heart? Why else would I wake with the memory of his warmth still wrapped around me? The tingling of his kiss still upon my lips? He **must** be real.

Even if he isn't, I choose the dream world over this waking world.

"My heart belongs to you alone. Come, let me show you my kingdom." He holds out his hand with a look of utter devotion. I eagerly put my hand in his and he pulls me too close, my chest just barely touching his torso.

His eyes rove my face and I can feel the heat of his desire. I gaze into his merry-green eyes for several long moments. He looks at my mouth. I press closer as he wraps his arms around me and dips his head to place the softest kiss on my lips, causing a slight intake of breath from me— surprised at the warmth of his body and the intensity of his scent.

He starts to draw back, but I follow him and hold his neck. Lifting myself to place a return kiss and just a hint of my tongue on his mouth. It is like I set a flame to an oil-soaked house, immediate chaos.

He crushes me to him, and I hold him equally fiercely. Both of us give in to our desires. Kissing between whispers and groans and whimpers— his and mine.

I wake to the sound of my phone alarm announcing that I must join the waking world. I roll over to snooze it. *A few more minutes, it was just getting good.* But consciousness has arrived completely to chase away any lingering sleep. I close my eyes, hoping to capture one last memory of my prince, but the fog of dreams is thick, recalling only green eyes and the warmth of his kiss. *Ah, well. That will have to be enough.*

Releasing a resigned sigh at having to leave my warm bed to be a responsible adult, I throw off my thin summer blanket and reach for the remote to switch on the TV. Overly cheery voices greet me with yet more news on the coming hazardous weather that is still many days away and speculations on whether it will be a tropical storm or become a hurricane by landfall.

I'm still lost in the memory of a particularly wonderful dream while going through my morning routine. The day is looking to be warm and humid but I still opt for black leggings and a comfortable t-shirt featuring a smiling sun that says "anxiety sucks." Throwing my cellphone, earbuds, inhaler, and NASA hoodie—it won't get chilly later but it's my comfort—into a tote bag. I grab an apple to eat during my walk to work at the library because, as usual, I woke up too late to have a proper breakfast.

I step out into the bright sunshine to find Daisy is already tending to her garden while a fat tuxedo cat sits on the patio chair, watching her efforts to make the plants grow strong. I press the lock on my side of the house, then walk over to pet Sylvestro for a few moments while Daisy greets me, "*Ciao*, Hrachuhi. I leave *pomodori* for you tonight."

I smile warmly, "Thank you. I will make sure they get eaten." *I hate tomatoes.* This has been my secret for the years I have lived here, my lovely landlady leaves tomatoes from her garden on my living room table and I pretend to eat them, but really, I bring them to coworkers and the occasional bird that crosses my path.

With a wave to Daisy, and one last stroke to the purring Sylvestro, I start the fifteen minute walk to work, taking bites of my apple while enjoying the music playing in one ear during my commute. I feel a bubble of joy form in my chest and I smile at the clear blue sky. You wouldn't know a storm is approaching.

Excerpt from Dancing for the Cold Moon

There is no point in going back to the guards tonight, the gates will be locked by now and there will be too many questions with all this blood on me. I dip the cloth in the sage and myrrh tea, doing my best to wash all of his blood off my skin.

The old woman leaves me a fat slice of bread drizzled generously with honey and some warm willow bark tea before rushing out again. I inhale the food, licking the darkly-sweet golden honey from my fingers. Sighing contentedly with a belly full and seated in the warm room, while being beyond exhausted, I start to nod off.

When the old woman at last returns, she brings more poultice, tea wash, and bandages. "I sleep now. Wake me if he dies." I jump like I have been slapped, no longer sleepy. "I leave him to you, I can do no more."

So I keep my vigil by his bedside. Washing his wounds and wrapping them with fresh poultices throughout the long night. I retrieve more well water to cool his forehead hoping to temper this fever and bring some comfort.

There are times in the night when he jerks and stretches and groans, gritting his teeth like he is in great pain. Those times I find myself holding his hand tightly in mine, running my fingers through his hair, whispering fervently and pleading with him to fight and live another day.

Just before daybreak, I fall into an exhausted sleep, still praying to the spirits with his name on my lips.

I half awaken to feel a hand stroking my hair causing me to sigh dreamily. The hand moves to caress my cheek and I unconsciously press my face into it, beginning to drift deeper into sleep for a few moments... when I realize this is no dream.

I open my eyes to find him caressing my cheek with his elegant fingers, his touch feather-light. He is staring at me with a look akin to wonder in his eyes. I sit straight up and his hand drops away.

His eyes are bright with fever and his skin is still flushed— he must not be in his right mind, I touch his forehead to find his skin burns hotly. I feel his burning gaze as he tracks me while I rush to prepare more tea, and then I coax him into drinking the entire cup.

He sets the cup down on the pallet and reaches for me; I sit very still— like a frightened rabbit without cover—and hold myself carefully away. "I dreamed of you. You had golden flowers woven into your hair and you gifted me a smile as radiant as the moon."

I look away because I do not want to hear these warm words— like drops of nectar in the sun spilling from his lips.

He attempts to speak more of his fever dream but I shush him, telling him he needs to rest quietly to promote faster healing.

I bathe his face with tepid water that is cooling to his feverish skin, gently touching his bruised and swollen face while ignoring his soft, gray eyes searching my face— seeking an answer for which I do not know the question.

At last, he falls into a deep sleep and I practically run out of the cottage, trying to escape the warmth of his eyes and the heat of his hand still on my cheek.

A word from the author

To all of my readers, however you obtained a copy of my work, whether it was purchased or borrowed via the library (please request it for free if you haven't already and please support your local library!) or other "unconventional" means, please remember that leaving a review/rating—good or bad—is free and always appreciated!

I hope you enjoyed this side story within the Celestial Sagas series. There is more to come, so keep an eye out on my social media: Terri4books on various platforms or Terri Rath.

I am a firm believer that representation matters. So, you will often find my stories will center around people of color, bodies of all shapes and sizes, mental disabilities, and neurodivergence. If you are disappointed by a lack of representation of yourself in my stories, please understand that I hesitate to write about topics that are not within my scope of in-depth knowledge because I fear accidentally offending or hurting any readers with unintended ignorance. Please know that I support everyone's right to live as their heart desires, and to not be bound by the expectations of societies with outdated mindsets.

I hope that somehow you are able to find a connection to my stories and my characters. Thank you for being here on my journey to change the narrative. Happy reading, lovelies!

About the Author

Terri Rath has lived her whole life with her head in the clouds while residing in Ohio. She is passionate about animals, mental health awareness, and music. Her perfect day is being cozied up at home during a storm with her loved ones and a mug of hot chocolate.

Now she is focused on sharing her stories with the world.

Find her on various social media platforms under: Terri Rath or Terri4books

Also by Terri Rath

A woman searching for her place in the human world. A prince hoping to reclaim his kingdom.

A Lingering Dream

"You have the power to change the dream, you need only reach for it."

She thought nothing of the men who loved her in the Dreaming, they were just the desires of her heart made tangible. But an idea grew into a suspicion. Could one of them be real?

Her dreams will lead her to discover a power that frees a Prince of the Waters and awakens an old enemy. It's up to the Lost Prince to protect her as she learns how to control her new powers.

The journey will lead them to uncover lost memories and a past life full of dark trauma, but they will also find a love that transcends lifetimes.

A Lingering Dream is an evocative, portal fantasy-romance with a dash of spice.

Dancing for the Cold Moon

"I close my eyes as terror floods my body because I know... he is coming for me."

Choose: A life of service or death?

An imprisoned woman is given the chance to pay for her crimes by becoming a soldier for the Kingdom to fight the demons that cross the veil. Encountering hardships as she navigates this new position of authority while trying to escape her brutal past, complications arise in the forms of the handsome Captain of the Guard and an audacious mercenary determined to bring her back to the darkness.

Dancing for the Cold Moon is a dark fantasy about the darkness within ourselves and the choices we make in the face of terrible abuses.